RUMORS

Erica Kiefer

Clean Teen Publishing

RUMORS

clean teen PUBLISHING

ISBN: 978-1-940534-87-9
Cover Design by: Marya Heiman
Typography by: Courtney Nuckels
Editing by: Cynthia Shepp

YA

Content Disclosure

For more information about our content disclosure, please utilize the QR code above with your smart phone or visit us at www.cleanteenpublishing.com.

To my father for his devotion to education and love of all things written, and to my mother for her relentless spirit and constant ability to find the light beyond the shadows.

CHAPTER ONE

Rumors—they spread fast like a virus, mutating and growing stronger with each person they touch. The difference between a rumor and virus, though, is that no one wants a virus. We do all we can to protect ourselves and to eradicate the spreading germ. On the other hand, the moment we get a taste of a rumor, we want more—taking pride in being the source of delivery. Fortunately, we can kill a virus with medicine. The only way to kill an infectious rumor, though, is to tell the truth—but if the truth hurts more than the rumor, perhaps it's better to let the rumor run rampant.

Rumors were the reason I often hid in the bathroom, avoiding the questioning eyes of my high school peers. It was definitely not the ideal way to start my senior year, but it was easier to hide than risk the questions. Besides, from my position inside the handicap stall, I sometimes overheard tidbits of scandal, like how this kid named Derek cheated on Anna, even though everyone swore at the beginning of summer that they were going to make it. Now everyone hates Noel because of it. Unfortunately, sometimes I couldn't escape playing the lead role in the circulating rumors, and all I could do was stand in that stall and listen.

All the stories, since school began two months ago, suggested I was in an accident. The details of this accident became hazy, depending on who shared them. Some tales were way off base and suggested I lost control of my four-wheeler and smashed my head into the ground. That would explain why I didn't say much to anyone about what happened. They chalked it up to partial amnesia. Others were adamant that I fell off a Jet Ski and was hit by a boat, rendering me unconscious. Most people, however, seemed to know that I almost drowned in a river. Word spread that my cousin fell in the river, too. Although, the difference between my cousin and me was that she drowned. Since this happened in California, nobody here in Portland knew my cousin. Nobody really cared. They just liked to watch me from a distance, talking about me like I was an animal on display. They thought I couldn't hear them whispering or catch them in my peripheral, gawking in pity, but I did.

Rumors aside, no one understood why I wouldn't talk about it—why I refused to clarify the details of the accident last summer. It was simple really. Like I said, rumors can hurt—but sometimes, the truth can hurt more.

CHAPTER TWO

"What do you mean, you quit?" Coach Robbins leaned forward in his chair, his large forearms resting on the edge of the desk.

I sighed. I knew he wouldn't make this easy. "I can't—I'm not playing basketball this year." With wavering eye contact, I fidgeted on the squeaky, plastic cushion beneath me, wishing the chair had wheels so I could roll my way out of the office.

Coach Robbins shook his head. He made visible efforts to maintain composure—a skill he often lacked on the court. Pausing, he took a deep breath and spoke again. "Allie, I know it's been a rough start to your senior year. I'm very sorry about your cousin drowning over the summer, and I can only imagine how hard that must be—but this is your year!" His hand swept to his Wall of Fame, pointing to a framed article. The headlines stated with boldness: "RISE OF THE COLLINS TRIO!"

I didn't need to skim last year's article to remember the highlights: Sisters Allie, Taylor, and Leah Collins dominate the court at Sectional Championship, but come up short.

Coach Robbins watched me, his eyes lighting up

as if he could still feel the thrill of last year's game—the screaming fans, cheering in both joy and agony as the scoreboard bounced back and forth, mercilessly playing with their heartstrings until the last second on the clock. My younger twin sisters, Taylor and Leah, were the rising stars of the year. Starting on the JV team as freshmen and then catapulting to the Varsity team for playoffs, they made an impressive debut for their first year of high school.

The second half of that championship game was the first time all three of us had been on the same court in a competitive game. It was like the basketball transformed into a ball of fire, shifting between our hands. We read each other's movements with an unspoken gift shared only amongst sisters, our natural skills heightened by each other's presence. Shot after shot, all three of us lit up the court, causing a surge of adrenaline amongst our teammates and the fans in the bleachers. We overcame a mountainous lead so quickly that Coach Robbins only real lament was that he hadn't put us together sooner. Though we had lost the game by two points, the burning in Coach Robbins' eyes peered with eagerness toward next season.

This season. The season I was refusing to be a part of.

Coach Robbins stood up as if our conversation was over. By the look on his face, he was probably still caught up in the memories. That and it was time for the first basketball practice of the season. I stood and he put a hand on my shoulder, his towering height stooping a bit to bring his face closer to my own lean, five-foot-seven frame. "You will be just fine. I'm sure you're still hurting now from your loss, and that's to be expected, but you'll forget all about it once you start playing again. Get going, Collins. Suit up for practice." He thumped my back twice, opening the door for me, and escorting me out of his office.

I almost bumped into my teammates and the other athletes who were shuffling towards the locker rooms. Tara Davis, one of my best friends, wrapped her arms around me in a tight squeeze, spinning us both around. "Start of the season!" she squealed, not catching on to the lack of mirrored delight on my face—or maybe she simply chose to ignore it. So many people seemed to do that these days. "We are going to kill it!" She linked arms with me, towing me towards the locker room. I glanced back at Coach Robbins, who gave me a nod of approval before grabbing the attention of our assistant coach. Already, our brief and useless conversation was forgotten. The locker room doors swung shut behind me.

Suicides—one basketball drill I excelled at. To the line and back, I sprinted, my lungs burning by the final set. Yet, I pushed through the pain, leading my teammates with the strength and endurance expected of a captain.

Never giving up.

All the running I'd invested in over the last couple of months since Maddie's death paid off, my fitness allowing bursts of speed as I dashed from one line on the court to the next. My sisters, Taylor and Leah weren't far behind my heels. Despite my own lack of motivation today, I couldn't help but be impressed by their young enthusiasm. They moved with proficiency and confidence, shouting out encouragement to our teammates, and driven to succeed. They were only sophomores, but they didn't let the age-gap inhibit their self-assurance. I coveted their ability to play like Maddie hadn't died—like nothing had changed. She was their cousin, too. Yet, I was the one that felt hindered. Changed. Like all the energy put into this practice was a—

Tara Davis slapped my rear as she spun around me. "Wake up, girl!" she said as I missed her pass. The ball rolled away on its own, careening towards the exit of the gym. My mouth opened in surprise, not because Tara had smacked my behind like I was a cow, but because somehow I'd zoned out, not realizing we'd moved onto passing drills. Tara grinned at me, her wide smile stretching across her face. "Grab the ball! Let's go!"

As a best friend and co-captain, I guess she had the right to order me around. I picked up my knees and jogged after the runaway ball.

Practice carried on with more passing and shooting drills, weaving the ball between us and making the shot. We weren't introduced to anything new or crazy—not yet, anyway. I had no doubt Coach had a number of tactics up his sleeve, with my sisters and me playing a dominant role. Normally, I would expect and crave nothing else, relishing in the attention. Today, however, I couldn't shake the feeling that somehow, none of this was as important as it used to be. Life—and death, for that matter—was suddenly so much bigger than basketball.

We half-limped out of the doors when Coach Robbins released us, feeling the wake-up call of a brand-new season.

CHAPTER THREE

"Come on! Say yes to Friday." Tara Davis jumped in my path, walking backwards to stay in front of me. Frowning at her persistence, I continued walking down the school hall, trying not to step on her toes.

"Tara, seriously—I'm not in the mood. I would be the worst date anyway." I brushed passed Tara, finally getting ahead of her feet. She grabbed my backpack, slowing me down until I came to a stop. I took a breath and released it loudly.

"Allie, please. *Please* do this for me." Her olive-green eyes pleaded into mine. "Don't best friends reserve the right for favors once in a while?" She bounced on her toes.

I sighed. Going on a double date this Friday had little appeal to me, especially after our first grueling week of basketball practice, but Tara had created what she called "the perfect set up" by organizing a date night. She'd had her eye on Austin Boyer since our junior year. As a key player on the boys' basketball team, he was quite the commodity, and any girl would count herself lucky to be in his knee-buckling presence. Not far behind "every girl's dream" was Austin's best friend, Shane Moretti—and my date, should I concede.

Tara couldn't get over how cool it would be if "best friends dated best friends" and better yet, that we all played basketball. In her words, this type of scenario would be the pinnacle of our high school experience.

I shouldn't have given in—I should have held my ground, but I felt like I was disappointing a lot of people these days with my often-glum mood. For instance, I hadn't felt any need to dress up for Halloween last week and opted to stay home and hand out candy instead.

"What are you, OLD?" Tara had said in disgust, shaking her head at me when she couldn't convince me to attend the haunted house with her and a few friends. Regardless of her criticism, ever since Maddie's death, I felt like my nerves were still too fragile. The last thing I needed was an evening where ghosts and monsters were glorified and praised for jumping out at me. I already felt like a phantom of myself anyway, unable to fully grasp the confidence and zest for life that I once maintained. Maybe if I faked having a good time this weekend, people would stop watching me for a major meltdown—and Tara would stop pelting me with her disapproving looks.

"Ok," I said, "Let's do it. *One* double date to help you and Austin on your path to true love—although, you know I don't believe in any of that—and then you're on your own." Tara jumped up and down, wrapping her arms around me.

"You are absolutely the best!" Her springy, sandy-blond hair bounced with her voice. "I will plan everything. Meet me at my house on Friday after practice, and the boys can pick us up from there."

I feigned a smile in return, wondering what I'd just gotten myself into.

Friday came too soon. After showering from basketball practice, I escaped the house as fast I could, still hearing my sophomore sisters swooning over the idea that I was going on a date with Shane. Mom seemed pleased that I finally had Friday night plans again.

Dressed in black cords and a green sweater that scooped around her neck, highlighting her defined collarbones, Tara finished applying her final strokes of blush. Her reflection smiled at me as she spun around, her lips painted in burgundy lip gloss. She eyed my skinny jeans and grey sweater.

"I hope you brought a coat," she said, slipping into knee-length boots. "It's gonna be cold outside!" I glanced out the window into the dimming light.

"You still haven't told me where we are going," I said. "And I have a feeling it's because I probably don't want to go." I folded my arms, waiting for her to deny it.

She grinned, pulling my arm towards her bedroom mirror and seating me in the vanity seat. "We're going to a corn maze." She ignored my attempts to slap at her hand while she forced my eyelid closed with her makeup brush.

"A corn maze?" I frowned at the thought of being trapped in an oversized labyrinth with Tara and two guys I barely knew. "We *are* going to freeze! Do I need to remind you that you have no sense of direction?" I blinked at my reflection, catching the shimmering, smoky purple that Tara added to my eyes. I had to admit that the purple shadow did brighten my hazel iris. It also highlighted my disapproving glare.

"Well," Tara said, knocking the clutter of makeup into her vanity drawer, "I wouldn't mind getting lost with Austin for a while." She grinned mischievously.

"Oh, come on, Tara," I protested. "You are *not* running off with Austin and leaving me with Shane." I barely knew the guy. I hoped he didn't have any plans for hiding in a corner with me somewhere.

"Allie, you'll be just fine. This is the last weekend the maze is even open, so just enjoy it!" The doorbell rang, interrupting Tara's poor attempt to console me.

Austin and Shane stood in the entryway, both looking sharp in faded jeans and fitted, long-sleeved shirts.

"Ladies!" Austin greeted, his eyes brushing along Tara's body as we descended the staircase. The confident way he carried himself demanded attention. His light-colored hair was cropped short on the sides, except for his perfectly gelled faux hawk. Shane smiled at me with a little more reserve, though everything else about him exuded the same self-assurance as his best friend. His shapely eyebrows accentuated his dark brown eyes. He, too, kept his black hair short, though gelled for texture in front.

"Thanks for picking us up," Tara said, her smile pushing through to her high cheekbones. She grabbed a scarf and swirled it around her neck in a fashionable manner.

"You ready to do this?" Shane asked me as Tara and Austin led the way out the door.

"Of course," I answered, too intimidated by his attractiveness to maintain eye contact for very long. My heart beat fast in my chest, nervous and unsettled. I hadn't been out with a guy since before summer vacation, and I couldn't help feeling like I was the odd one in the group, lacking the confidence that radiated off each of them. Perhaps last year I would have felt differently—like I belonged—but now… I second guessed myself and assumed the worst when eyes roved towards me.

The car ride was fairly painless, since Austin drove with the bass bumped so high that we couldn't hold a conversation even if we wanted. Hip-hop blared from his speakers, rocking the inside of the car with upbeat sound waves. Shane and I sat in the back and the most we could do was holler a few superficial questions at each other, exchanging awkward smiles and head nods along the way. It was evident from the start that we were both going along for the ride for the sake of our best friends. We knew there was no interest between the two of us, despite Tara swearing up and down that she'd heard

Shane asking about me.

We stopped at a diner for a quick bite to eat, ordering drinks and burgers. We started off with easy conversation, exchanging the woes of killer basketball practices this week and our excitement for the first game. I tried to hold up my end of the conversation, but I noticed Shane's wandering eyes scoping out every cute girl that passed by our table, including the young waitress, her long legs suctioned to her tight pants. It wasn't that I was jealous. So far, other than striking features and a toned body, he didn't have much else to offer in personality—but whether I was interested or not, it never felt good to be on a date where the guy was checking out everyone else.

Tara and Austin hit it off, flirting back and forth, talking comfortably with one another. I really didn't know why they needed Shane and me as an excuse to go out. They were doing just fine on their own.

When we arrived at the corn maze, the night air threatened to seep through our coats. Though I was somewhat used to the damp cold—having moved to Portland for my sophomore year, I wasn't too keen on the idea of being stuck in this chilly air if we couldn't find our way out of the maze quickly.

Tara clung to Austin's elbow as he escorted her through the entrance. Shane and I followed behind, our efforts to find something to talk about dwindling. Two people could only talk so much about basketball and the weather.

"It's spooky in here," Tara commented after we had been walking for a minute. The dim lighting did cast odd shadows amid the tall cornstalks. "I love it!"

"Ever been through the corn maze when it's haunted?" Austin asked, pausing as we came to a crossroads. He shrugged at our options and guided us to the right.

"We went last year," I said, remembering the laughter and screams Tara and I had shared as we tore away from the scarecrow, who was hunting us down with his blaring chainsaw. I ended up tripping over a fallen cornstalk and cowering in a heap on the ground, while the scarecrow's chainsaw came terrifyingly close to my torso. Tara laughed as she retold the story to Austin and Shane, and I couldn't help but chuckle, too. Last year was full of memorable times, back when I had nothing to worry about and no heavy emotions weighing me down.

After ten minutes, we made some headway through the maze, though we'd also gone in circles a couple of times.

"How about we switch things up?" Austin asked, stopping at another intersection.

"What are you suggesting?" Shane asked.

Austin smiled at Tara. "I say we split up and make it a race to the end. Losers buy hot chocolate."

I cringed inside, but not wanting to be a poor sport, nodded in agreement. Shane seemed equally reluctant, given his expression, but he agreed. "Game on, man. Get ready to be schooled!"

Tara grinned eagerly, still latched to Austin's arm. "Catch you later, Allie." She leaned into my side and whispered, "Don't get *too* lost, if you know what I mean." I rolled my eyes, pretty sure that Tara and Austin planned on taking their time through the maze tonight and doing just that. They took off to the left. Alone for the first time, Shane left the decision up to me. "Where do you want to go?" he asked. "Straight ahead or turn right?"

Home, I thought, but kept my true opinion to myself. I stifled a yawn, trying to hide my disinterest behind one hand. "I don't know. You choose."

Shane frowned, perhaps disappointed with my lack of enthusiasm. "Well, I don't care either."

We both stood there without speaking for a few moments. Awkward and no fun, there was little point to this date anymore. I'd had enough of this charade. "Ok, can we both just be honest about this for a minute?"

Shane raised his eyebrows at my sudden change in tone.

"Neither of us wants to be here—I think that's fairly obvious."

Shane motioned like he was about to object, but I cut him off.

"Seriously, it's ok. You don't have to pretend that you want to be here." *It's not like you were doing a good job pretending anyway,* I added in my head.

Shane folded his arms. "All right, so neither of us wanted to come. Now what?"

I was a bit taken back by his statement, even

though I had assumed it to be true. "First of all, why *did* you come then?" I asked, folding my own arms against the chill. I wobbled my legs back and forth to keep warm. Dark clouds were rolling in with the increasing wind, further darkening the maze and adding to the cold.

He hesitated with his response, scratching the back of his head as he glanced down the row of corn where Austin and Tara had disappeared. "Because," he started, "I *was* a little bit interested in you," he paused before adding, "*last* year."

"Oh," I murmured, interpreting what he meant. *Last year,* when I had it all together as a rising basketball star with cool friends who hadn't tapered off from my life yet. I shook my head in dismay. So many people didn't know how to respond to this aching part of me, so they just avoided me altogether—even guys like Shane who apparently had crushes on me—the old me. My eyes met Shane's, and I tried not to feel hurt that I'd turned into someone less appealing, at least according to his words.

"So why did *you* come then?" Shane asked, his features showing his discomfort in our conversation.

"For Tara," I said. "She thought it'd be easier to hang out with Austin if we tagged along, but—"

Shane finished my sentence. "—but they're doing just fine without us." He nodded. "Ok, I can appreciate the honesty. We, uh, are still stuck in this maze, so we better get moving if we want to get out of here." He glanced at our options.

"Let's just go this way." Annoyed with the whole

evening, I strut off with long strides.

"Hey, Allie—" Shane's voice sounded contrite. He caught up to me, his footsteps moving quickly to keep up.

I could just kill Tara, I thought, blaming her for leaving Shane and me in an embarrassing situation.

"Just forget it," I said, not wanting to hear any fake apologies—not that he had anything to apologize for. He was forced into this awkward situation, too. I was just irritated and embarrassed. Shane sighed, following just a step behind me. Directionless, we meandered through the corn maze. We hit more dead ends than anything and bumped into less people. At this point, we had probably hit the outskirts of the maze on the wrong side of the finish line.

Light rain began its descent, dampening our clothes with its gentle, but steady fall.

As if this night could get any worse.

After a few more minutes of uncertainty in our steps, Shane grabbed my arm, halting my movement. "I have an idea. We need to see where we are. Come on, climb up." He lowered his body and offered me his back.

I raised an eyebrow. "What," I began, "are you talking about? I'm not climbing on you. I play basketball—I don't do cheerleading." I observed the growing mud beneath my boots. "Besides, my boots are filthy."

Shane rolled his eyes. "I don't care about the mud. Just get over here. I'm going to lift you up so you can see where we're at. We need a vantage point."

I groaned, knowing he was right. This maze was taking forever and with the wrong company. I straddled his neck so that I sat on top of his shoulders. He held onto my legs to provide more balance. Standing up, his six-foot height propelled me into the air.

"Whoa!" I gripped the top of his head in my hands when I swayed backwards.

Shane grunted. "Can you try not to gouge my eyes out?"

"Oops, sorry." Balanced at last, I removed my fingers from his face. Now that I could see above the cornstalks, I had an idea where we were. We had indeed cornered ourselves in the far side of the maze and needed to make our way up and to the left.

"Ok, I think we can do this," I said, tapping Shane's shoulder to signal for him to let me down. He bent his knees, and I slid off. "Let's go this way." I pulled his forearm after me, letting go once he followed.

"See, not a bad idea, right?" Shane stepped next to me as we moved.

"All right, I'll give you that one," I grudgingly said, though I smiled.

Shane returned a boastful grin and then glanced up at the sky, blinking away droplets. "We better pick up the pace."

We were so far off track that we continued to cheat our way through the maze, Shane lifting me to his shoulders a few more times to speed up the process. The rain followed us, an unrelenting drizzle. As we closed in on the finish, I couldn't help but let out a cry of satisfaction and joy.

"Yes, we made it!" I broke into a run, and Shane followed suit. Just as we rounded the corner, I lost my footing in a slick patch of mud and fell back onto my rear. I landed hard, mud sinking into my jeans.

I groaned, accepting Shane's hand as he pulled me to my feet. Embarrassed, I examined my behind, swiping at the mud. A couple of people in the distance pointed and laughed. I scowled at them, only too familiar with those gestures.

"*Of course* this would happen. Just stupid, muddy, icing on the cake," I grumbled under my breath. When I peeked at Shane to see if he was laughing too, my jaw dropped. He had removed his jacket and was in the process of pulling off his long-sleeved shirt.

"What are you—it's raining!" I pointed out, thrown off when I caught sight of his toned torso dripping in front of me. He handed me his shirt.

"Here," he offered, glancing at my mud-stained behind. "For your—err—"

"Oh... thanks." I tied his sleeves around my waist so that his shirt covered my butt. I let out a laugh at the situation while Shane pulled his jacket back on, his body releasing a shiver. "Hot chocolate sounds pretty good right now," I said. "I don't care who's buying!"

Shane chuckled. "Come on." He placed his hand on my back to guide me forward. "Let's get out of here."

CHAPTER FOUR

I sat up in bed, gasping. Damp with sweat, my oversized T-shirt clung to my skin. My eyes frantically scanned my surroundings, desperate to be calmed by familiarity.

My white, three-drawer dresser stood across the room, spilling its contents over the brim of each drawer. My phone and iPod lay on the desk. I felt the queen bed beneath me, the quilt and sheets twisting around my legs like snakes. With a shaky hand, I grabbed my phone. It was three in the morning.

My breathing slowed as I tried to forget the images from my reoccurring nightmare. I untangled the bedding from my body and slid off the mattress. Walking into the bathroom that joined my room with my twin sisters', I peeked at them. Both were sound asleep in their separate beds, Taylor snoring softly. I envied their peaceful slumber, not remembering the last time I slept hard enough to snore. Gently, and with a muffled sigh, I closed the door and flipped on the bathroom light.

I groaned as I saw my reflection in the mirror. The dark layers of my hair curled around my narrow face in a wiry, tangled mess. The hint of green in my hazel eyes appeared paler this morning, dimmed and resentful at the forced awakening, and the dark smudges of yesterday's makeup darkened the bags under my eyes.

Twisting the faucet, I let the cool water cascade from the spout onto my hands. Still dazed from perpetual lack of sleep, my mind zoned in on the falling water, eyelids heavy. The water sounded like a stream, rushing and gurgling. Or like a river… In the next moment, the water seemed thunderous in my ears, like a waterfall—overwhelming me, triggering the memories from my nightmare—or more accurately, from last summer's reality.

Arms flailing, my head popped up, and I inhaled both air and water. Choking and sputtering, my lungs burned. The icy current absorbed my whole body once again as the river dipped, its cruel waters knocking me into hidden boulders. I bobbed up and down, a mere puppet in the water's clutches. My bones and cold muscles ached for relief. My own cries echoed in my ears.

Catching hold of brush protruding from the embankment, my fingers weaved into the thick growth. I searched for her, my own grip slipping.

Then I heard Maddie's scream…

"Allie! Honey, wake up!"

Maddie wasn't screaming. I was screaming.

My eyes focused on Mom and then I felt her firm grip on my left shoulder, while her other hand cupped my face.

"There you go. Good girl. You're ok," Mom said.

"Everything is ok..."

I inhaled and exhaled too quickly, feeling light-headed while trying to divide the nightmare from memories—but the line was too thin.

"Slow down, honey. Deep breaths..."

I let out a sob and Mom pulled me close, wrapping her arms around me.

"I'll get some water," Leah said, a tired hand rubbing across her eyes. She exited her bedroom. It was only then that I realized the door connecting the bathroom to her bedroom was open. I pulled away from Mom, wiping my eyes and sucking back the tears. I saw Taylor sitting up in bed, her head resting on folded arms on top of her knees. I heard her release a soft groan.

My screams had woken up the household. Again.

"I'm sorry," I mumbled, rubbing my face with both hands.

"Come on, Allie." Mom guided me back to bed and straightened out my bedding.

With my tears sealed back in place, I said, "I'm fine, Mom. Sorry I woke everyone. Just go back to bed. I'm ok." I put a hand on hers, trying to prevent her from fluffing my pillow anymore.

She sat down beside me. "Are you, Allie? Are you fine? Because I don't think so."

"Mom, please..." I knew where this was going.

"I don't want to rush you through the process," Mom said with a shake of her head, "but you need help. If you won't talk to us, then you *need* to talk to a therapist or the school counselor… *somebody.*"

"Mom…" My eyes welled up, exhaustion and embarrassment catching up with me. I didn't want to have this conversation again. I didn't want to talk at all. If I had to speak about it, then that made it an issue, and I didn't want to have issues. I just needed to believe it would all go away with time.

"Here, Allie." Leah handed me a cup of water.

"Thanks," I said, glad for the interruption.

"Sure. I'm going back to bed, ok? We have that sprint test today and if I'm going to compete with you, I need my sleep." She offered a closed smile, followed by a yawn.

I nodded, and she returned to her room. Avoiding eye contact with Mom, I stared at the water in my cup. Silence grew between us until a quiet sigh from Mom made me glance at her.

She ran a hand through her blonde hair. "Allie, I'm trying to do the right thing here. How long do I let this go on? You can't face this on your own."

"I don't need special help, Mom." I could feel burning emotion growing inside, but I tried to smother it from within. "We all lost somebody. Maddie was Leah and Taylor's cousin, too. She's your niece. Why am I the only one that needs help?"

"You were in that river, too, Allie. I know you haven't forgotten that." She gestured towards the bathroom and back at me. "You *obviously* haven't forgotten that. Maybe all these bad dreams are because you are keeping everything inside you. It's not healthy!" Mom's voice rose, touched with a quiver of tears. "We all love Maddie. We all miss her, and each of us has our bad days. But Allie—I don't even know how to say this without making you feel bad—" Mom paused, looking towards my window for a moment. I swallowed the building lump in my throat, anticipating her words. "We are all hurting, and probably always will to some degree. But you are struggling more than anyone else is. I see you pulling away from everyone. I never thought I'd say this, especially with you leaving for college next fall... but I want you out of the house more! Why don't you hang out with your friends? Why are you running so much? Why don't you talk about basketball like you used to?"

I frowned, clenching the sheets in my fists. "I just need time. Just... more time. No one said I needed to get over Maddie's death in five months."

"I didn't say get over it, Allie. But you can't just let time pass and do nothing. *Please*, talk to somebody. To start with, at least hang out with your friends again. You need people in your life." Mom paused before adding, "Your dad would kill me for encouraging this, but what about that boy from last night?"

She was getting desperate. I closed my eyes. I would not allow her to bring Shane or any other boy into this part of my life.

Mom released an audible breath. She spoke once more, softly and with a touch of surprise. "Allie, when did you take all your pictures off the wall?" I could hear the sadness in her voice—her disappointment.

Mom seemed to be waiting, watching… minutes passed, but I kept my eyes pulled shut until she left my room without another word. When I heard the door close, I sat up and stared at my mostly bare walls. There were a couple of posters of my favorite alternative rock bands and movies, but the photo collages that used to be taped across my wall were gone. I opened the bottom drawer of my desk, tugging a couple of times when the drawer became stuck from the overflowing pictures. The top photos slid onto the floor. Gingerly, I picked up three and sifted through them. The first was of my sisters and me in our basketball jerseys, faces flushed from last year's Sectional Championship. I stood in the center of them, my arms embracing Leah and Taylor on either side, our expressions happy despite our close loss. In the second picture, a blonde, nine-year-old girl beamed at the camera, her brilliant blue eyes shining under the sun. I was lying next to her on the inflated tube, my hair hanging in wet strands around my face. Both of us were wrapped in life jackets. It was the last picture I'd taken with Maddie, only days before she drowned.

The rest of the drawer was full of basketball photos and my favorite vacation memories, most of them from our time at Hidden Pines. More pictures of Maddie surfaced, and I remembered why these photos were hidden away. After last week's nightmare, I'd ripped them all down—not ready to throw them away, but unable to bear the images that taunted me of my past life.

CHAPTER FIVE

Walking to my locker on Monday, I caught sight of Shane and his basketball buddies walking down the hall. Remembering my fall at the corn maze, I tried to avoid him by finding someone—anyone—to talk to, but everyone around me was already preoccupied in conversation or fiddling with their lockers. Despite the laugh we'd shared in the moment, seeing Shane surrounded by all his arrogant guy friends pushed any familiarity aside.

I pulled out my phone and pretended to be thoroughly absorbed in texting, my feet still carrying me forward. No text in the history of texting ever required so much concentration.

"I'll catch up with you guys later," I heard Shane's voice say as I passed him and his posse of testosterone. I picked up the pace and rounded the corner of the hall. Shane's hand on my shoulder pulled me to a stop.

"Allie, hey," Shane said. I glanced at his hand on my shoulder—which he quickly removed—before I looked up at him. As usual, he wore jeans and a tight, long-sleeved shirt, reminding me of the muddied one I returned to him on Friday night. I dropped my eyes, blushing at the memory of totally eating it at the corn maze.

The night had ended pretty quickly after that. Tara and Austin had been waiting for us for over twenty minutes—though I noticed Tara's lip gloss needed a touch up, so I was sure they'd found ways to keep busy. We grabbed some hot chocolate but drank it in the car on our way home. Considering my wet and muddy jeans and Shane missing his shirt, hanging out any longer wasn't really an option. Besides, I could tell Tara was dying to know if there was more to the story as to why Shane had removed his shirt. She seemed thoroughly disappointed with the humiliating truth of the matter.

"Hi," I said to Shane, almost in question.

"Listen, I just want to apologize about Friday night."

"Why? It's not like you pushed me down or anything." I tried to lighten the conversation with a laugh.

"No, that's not what I'm talking about." Shane's eyes became more serious. "I didn't mean to hurt your feelings when I said—"

I cut him off before our conversation could take that awkward turn. I did *not* want to relive that part of our discussion where he basically told me I was not that interesting anymore. "It's not a big deal," I said, taking a step back to distance myself from him. The bell rang, warning me that I had five minutes to get to class. I looked around the hallway, which was quickly becoming void of students. I took another anxious step backwards.

I hated walking into class late, winning more unwanted attention.

Shane seemed like he had more to say, his mouth opening and closing like he couldn't decide on his words.

I made it easy on him by waving goodbye, looking over my shoulder with a fleeting, "I'll talk to you later!"

After basketball practice, my sisters and I stayed late to hit the weight room. While the extra routine wasn't required, Coach had made a point of highly recommending strength training. As I entered the small weight room, I caught sight of Shane among the male athletes. He lifted his chin in greeting, putting down the dumbbells and pausing between sets. I acknowledged him with a brief wave of my hand.

Taylor quieted a squeal from her position beside me. "He is *so* hot," she said, trying to casually check Shane out. Beads of sweat slid down his defined biceps, exposed from the athletic tank top he wore. Taylor and Leah walked with me to the mats on the floor, each of us grabbing a medicine ball.

"Are you going to go out with him again?" Leah asked, her eyes roaming the gym as she checked out the older high school athletes sauntering into the room.

"On another date? Nope, that's definitely not happening again," I answered, lying on my back and holding the medicine ball in my hands. "Other than basketball, we have nothing in common. Not that I'm interested anyway… Hey, are you two going to do abs with me, or are you just here to check out the buffet?" My sisters snickered, taking one more glance around the room before joining me on their backs.

Gripping the weighted ball, I partnered with Taylor for sit-ups, tossing it back and forth. Leah twisted from side to side, working her obliques. After less than a minute, she said, "Dad called last night." Her eyes carefully watched my face.

I grunted, returning my focus to the ball. "And?"

I heard Leah sigh. "And he's wondering if you're ever going to return his phone calls."

I heaved the ball harder than necessary, causing Taylor to overextend her reach to catch it. "Hey!" She retrieved the ball. "Come on, Allie, watch it."

I sat up, resting my hands on my knees. "Sorry, Tay." To Leah, I said, "What'd you tell him?"

"Just that you had a lot of homework and would call him later. As usual," she added. I caught her disapproving gaze, which made me feel guilty but also irritated.

"I wish he'd just stop trying so hard," I said, not really expecting a response. We'd had this conversation too many times. Still, it didn't stop Leah from commenting.

"He's our *dad,* Allie. He made a mistake. How long are you going to hold it against him?"

"I don't hate him, Leah. You know we get along fine during visits—for the most part. I just don't feel like being best buddies with him." I stood up, hoping to end the conversation.

"Ok, whatever," she said. "Just passing on the message."

"I'll catch him next time or something," I muttered. Dumbbells in hand, I stepped across the floor with low lunges, again not understanding how my sister's reactions to our life circumstances could vary so differently from mine. Our complicated relationship with Dad aside, I was still trying to adjust to our differences over Maddie's death. As close as we were on the basketball court, dealing with Maddie's absence in our lives had already wedged a gap of misunderstanding between us. Leah and Taylor were there, too, at our summer cabin when Maddie died; yet somehow, their lives didn't seem as hindered as mine did. I often sensed their frustration with me.

Leah and Taylor's seemingly faster recovery from Maddie's passing reminded me of when Dad left Mom. I was not yet thirteen the summer when Dad's secret fling caught up with him. Leah and Taylor's forgiving nature allowed him back into their lives with more ease than I allowed him back into mine. What was wrong with me that I struggled more than they did in both situations? The burning in my quadriceps broke me from my contemplation. Grateful for the distraction, I moved on to the next exercise.

Shane came over while I concentrated on my triceps, pulling down the bar from my seated position. "Not bad, Collins," he said, eying the cut in my lean muscles. I blew out air with each pull, trying not to appear self-conscious. He waited for me to finish my set. I released the bar, stretching my right arm across my body.

"Can I help you?" I asked, catching my breath. I swiped a loose strand of hair away from my face, tucking it behind my ear.

"Hostile," Shane commented with an amused look. "I like it."

"Hostile—what are you talking about? I'm just in the middle of something." I stood up to lessen the height difference between us. At five-seven, I was short for a basketball player and had to make up for it with speed and endurance.

"'In the middle of something', like that super-important text this morning before class?" Shane's mouth hinted at a smile. He was teasing me.

"I was totally texting!" I lied. I hated that he'd noticed my discomfort. "What's it to you, anyway?"

Shane shrugged. "Nothin'. I just think it's interesting that you've been avoiding me all day."

"I haven't been avoiding you. It's not like we have classes together or anything." I paused for a moment. "What's with the sensitivity?" I asked, fully aware that Taylor and Leah were gawking at us from across the room, giggling to each other.

Ugh, sophomores.

"Well, you know, it's hard on a guy's self-esteem when you go on a date and the girl snubs you."

"It was hardly a date. You and I both know we were forced into unnecessarily chaperoning two friends."

Tara and Austin were together right now, spending every bit of their free time at school and now after practice. I was pretty sure I wouldn't be seeing much of my best friend anymore, aside from our structured basketball practices.

Shane stretched his arms above his head. "Well, I don't like having a black mark on my record. How about a do-over?"

"You want to go out again?" I didn't do a good job of hiding the shock in my voice.

"Yeah, why not? Just so we can say we had one good date. It'll help my confidence."

I rolled my eyes. This guy didn't need any help in the confidence department, and he knew it. He didn't break eye contact while he silently pressured me for an answer. "Ok, what did you have in mind?"

"Well, the boys' and girls' varsity team is coming over to my place on Friday. It's a bit of short notice, but we're trying to spread the word. If our teams are going to join forces and sell those raffle tickets together for Sectionals, some of the guys and I were thinking we might want to invest in some co-ed bonding."

I tried not to laugh at what else that might entail.

"That's your idea of a date? Hanging out with our basketball teammates?"

Shane laughed. "No, but that's where we can start. We'll do something afterwards."

I shrugged. It sounded harmless enough, though I wasn't sure where this was going. Still, the teenager in me couldn't help but feel happy that Shane was making an effort to talk to me, despite the flop of our first date. "Sure. I'll see you there." I returned to my triceps, ignoring my whispering twin sisters from across the room.

Based on the extravagant drive through Shane's gated community, with the security guard checkpoint and all, I shouldn't have felt the need to gawk at his spacious and equally impressive backyard. Tall lampposts lit up the field of grass, illuminating the trees bordering the yard. A paved pathway wound around the outskirts in a circular formation. Tables and chairs sat in the center, the tables displaying an assortment of finger foods. Bottled sodas packed with ice lay in huge buckets beside the tables.

"Shane's pad is so cool," Tara said in awe. "Remind me to marry a brain surgeon like Shane's dad when I grow up."

"No kidding," I agreed, "Check out the fire pit!" In the corner of the yard, theater-style seating allowed us to step down into the fire pit, approaching the cluster of students roasting marshmallows around the huge, concrete ring. Upbeat music set the energetic mood of the party, with kids laughing and dancing to the tempo.

"There's Austin." Tara's smile broadened, and she ran a hand through her straightened hair, her natural curls flat-ironed smooth today. "I'll see you later," she said to me, practically skipping over to him. I watched

Austin open his arms to her, swirling her around in a big hug. Tara threw her head back with a laugh. She made dating look so easy.

Scoping out the rest of the party, I caught sight of my sisters standing together at the edge of the fire. While they weren't identical, their features closely resembled each other enough that they were often mistaken for one another—both with the same nutty-brown hair like mine, though Leah recently cut hers short and angled by her chin and Taylor's long locks maintained golden highlights.

Like their hair, their social confidence outside of basketball differed as well. Leah's arms were wrapped around herself for warmth, though the way her eyes darted through the crowd with a half-smile on her face, I knew she was nervous to be at her first varsity party. She looked a little starstruck surrounded by the older athletes. Taylor, on the other hand, appeared to dominate the conversation with Grant, a decent player from the boys' team, who was chatting with her. She spoke with the self-assurance that Leah often lacked in large social settings, though I knew both of them would do just fine. Their own rise in stardom as the newest and youngest Collins gave them a head start in the social arena.

Two hands squeezed my shoulders from behind. Startled, I whipped around. The culprit grinned back at me, his brown eyes catching the light from the fire. Facing Shane, I couldn't help noticing that his red sweatshirt contrasted nicely with his warm skin tone.

"Thought you might not show," he said.

I frowned at him. "Now why would you say that?"

"Because you've basically turned into a hermit since school started." He seemed to regret his words the moment they slipped out of his mouth. "Oh, I mean—"

I sighed. What he meant was to say was, "Since your cousin drowned and you became socially reclusive." I remembered why I'd been avoiding these gatherings. People always said the wrong things, even when their intentions were good.

I put my fingers against Shane's mouth, blocking any more of his fumbling words. "You really could work on your tact. Do you always say the first thing that pops into your head?"

Shane's eyes scanned my features. He half-smiled and said, "Obviously not. Because if I did, the first thing I would have said to you is how pretty you look tonight." He brushed a layer of hair away from my eyes.

My mouth opened, but now I was the one struggling for words. Shane maintained his unnerving gaze. I settled for clearing my throat, taking a moment to break eye contact. He was flirting with me, and I wasn't sure how I felt about it. One date gone horribly wrong, and now he was being charming?

I forced a laugh, attempting to act casual, like I wasn't picking up on his flirtatious vibe. I was sure it didn't mean anything, anyway. Guys like Shane could say whatever they wanted and get away with it, even if they didn't mean what they said.

Since I was at a loss for a witty response, I changed the subject entirely. "So… did you sell any raffle tickets this week?"

Shane let out a chuckle, though since I hadn't said anything the least bit funny, I knew it was directed at me. "You want to talk about the raffle?" Amusement touched his expression.

My cheeks burned. I hoped that even with the lighting from the moon that he wouldn't notice the sudden pink hue. First he was rude, then charming, and then back to making fun of me? I couldn't figure him out, and I didn't like it. I let out a frustrated huff of air, looking through the crowd for an escape. Talking to Shane was impossible because, for whatever reason, he set my nerves on edge. I could barely hold a decent conversation with the guy, whether it was because of his good looks or dumb, insensitive comments.

Shane's fingers lightly touched my elbow until I looked back at him. He probably sensed my irritation because his features dropped the hint of mockery. "Come on, let's get out of here."

"To where?" I asked, slightly heated. "On our *date?*" My tone indicated that if this was the start of our evening, I was less than impressed.

"Follow me," he said. "Let's go for a walk." He took a few steps and then turned around, waiting for me.

Stalling, my eyes found my sisters, both of them now comfortably seated on the iron chairs beside the fire. They were smiling and heavily involved in the conversation at play with a group of guys. Tara was nowhere to be found—and neither was Austin, so I could guess her whereabouts clearly enough. Aside from a couple of friendly smiles and fleeting waves from my teammates (who paused their conversations only long enough to briefly acknowledge me), I was on my own.

With nothing better to do, I shoved my cold hands into the pockets of my white coat and caught up to Shane. We ascended the stairs out of the fire pit. In silence, Shane led me to the corner of the yard. He lifted the lock and pushed the double doors of the gate open, closing it behind us.

We walked without speaking for a couple of minutes, our shoes padding against the cool sidewalk beneath us. Since Shane had pretty much laughed at me when I had tried to start a conversation earlier, I refused to initiate. However, he didn't seem bothered by the silence. I caught him glancing at me a time or two, a mostly hidden smile in his expression. He'd look away when I'd make eye contact, but only after making sure our eyes did, in fact, meet for a moment.

After cutting through Shane's ornate neighborhood, I could see we were approaching an enormous, luscious golf course. Some of it was well lit by huge floodlights, probably for security, while dimmer areas relied on moonlight.

"So, what do you think?" Shane asked, taking in the view from beside me.

It was the most gorgeous golf course I'd ever seen.

"I can't believe you have your very own golf course inside your neighborhood." Disbelief etched in my voice. It wasn't like I grew up without money or anything. I knew Dad spoiled us, too—sometimes, it seemed to be his way to make up for the divorce. Even still, to have this huge golf course in the center of your community was unreal.

Shane stepped onto the perfectly groomed grass. I followed.

"Are we allowed out here?" I asked, looking around at the quiet course void of people.

"Of course not," Shane answered, his steps unfaltering. "But, are you seeing this place? It's huge. They can't watch all of it at the same time. Come on."

We trailed quietly, ditching the homes behind us and delving deeper into the golf course. Passing through a few hills, we situated ourselves on top of one mound with a gathering of trees. Hiding in the shadows, I pulled my knees up to my chest for warmth, resting my arms around my knees. The huge lake before us added to the quiet peace.

I gave in and broke the silence. "So, do you golf? I would guess yes since it's practically your backyard."

"Nah, not so much. I've tagged along with my dad and his country club buddies now and then, but golf's not really my thing. It's too slow—too structured."

"So maybe mini-putt is more your style?"

"Ha! Mere child's play." Shane leaned back onto his hands. "Yeah, I don't mind it. If I had a choice, I'd rather hit the driving range. I come with the guys sometimes.

Although, when we all come to the golf course, we tend to get a little more *creative* than the average golfer." I thought I caught a mischievous grin play across his face, but it disappeared before I could be sure.

"I wonder how many golf balls would be found in the lake if someone drained it?" I pictured the thousands of golfers who had run this course over time. I knew if I came out here, that was where most of my golf balls would end up.

"Good question. Let's go find out," Shane said. He jumped to his feet. Grabbing my hand, he pulled me up.

I dug my feet into the ground when he tried tugging me down the hill. "What? No way!" I shouted, though a laugh escaped my protest. Shane's hand covered my mouth, his body stepping into mine.

"Shh! Do you want us to get caught?"

With muffled objections, I reached up with both my hands, pulling on his forearm to make him release me. He chuckled, not letting go.

Ok, he asked for it.

Twisting my face, I bit his finger—hard.

"Ow!" Shane pulled his hand away, shaking his right hand and examining his finger. "You're a little beast!" Despite his amused tone, I knew the bite must have hurt.

I grinned wickedly in satisfaction. "That'll teach you to put your hands on me like that," I said.

"You're a fighter," Shane concluded, shaking his head at me. "That's good. It'll get you far in life."

I dropped my smile, his choice of words hitting home.

Fighter.

That's how everyone described me after the drowning accident last summer.

"*It's a good thing she's a fighter,*" I heard everyone say at the hospital when I pretended to be asleep, not wanting to face anyone or answer any questions. "*She could have died, too.*"

I *was* a fighter. I knew I'd put up a good fight against the tumultuous river—but so had Maddie. She had more fight in her than I did. She should have survived. If only I hadn't—

"Allie..." Shane ventured closer, noticing my sudden change in demeanor. I knew what he could see—the emotionally broken parts of me displayed on my face, weighing heavily on my shoulders. My posture would appear slightly hunched, as if I struggled to carry a load—and my hazel eyes, most of all, would be void of the glistening laughter from moments ago. I knew how I looked because I'd seen those sorrowful eyes, accusing me from my own reflection, for months.

"I'm sorry." Confusion touched Shane's voice. "What did I say?"

I shook my head, my eyes casting to the ground. He was oblivious to the impact of his words, not even considering that Maddie often occupied my thoughts. Memories of the accident often hit me out of nowhere. It wasn't Shane's fault. Like everyone else, he lived a sheltered life—and I didn't mean from a worldly standpoint. He had never experienced the hurt and pain I was suffering, so he couldn't relate. No one could.

No, it wasn't his fault at all. Shane's life was void of the emotional devastation that comes from loss—from guilt. He was just an average senior in high school, a typical jock juggling academics, athletics, and girls, whose biggest worry was which college he would attend. I couldn't expect more of him, and so I would not even try to pull him into my disparaging world.

I forced a tight-lipped smile. "Nothing." My voice was a whisper, pushing past my emotions. I pulled out my phone and checked the screen. "I… just remembered I was supposed to drive my sisters home thirty minutes ago." I let out a breath of air, playing the part. "Mom's gonna kill me. She didn't want them at the party too long." My eyes wouldn't meet Shane's. I didn't know if he believed me or if he could see past my strained façade.

I also didn't expect his soft lips to touch my forehead, or for him to place his hand on the back of my neck, pulling me closer.

My breath caught in my chest, confused and uncertain. Shane's lips lingered on my skin before he lowered his forehead to mine. I closed my eyes, uncertain if Shane's eyes were closed as well, or if he was watching my tentative reaction.

Either way, I didn't see him make his move. I only felt him place his fingers beneath my chin, lifting my face. His lips touched mine, ever so softly—almost in question, like he was testing my response. My mouth opened slightly, perhaps about to protest. I didn't know for sure because the next moment, before I could decide if my heart was drumming faster from attraction or nervousness, Shane moved his mouth more adamantly to mine. His hand slid to the side of my face, holding me steady.

I surrendered.

His kiss became our kiss. A shiver ran down my body, igniting a fuse of emotions—like a breath of fresh air blowing away the heaviness. In that moment, I forgot about my pain, and my guilt. All thoughts of Maddie were pushed aside.

For the first time in months, I felt sheltered.

CHAPTER SIX

Shane's kiss was the first thing I remembered when I awoke in bed Saturday morning. I had replayed the scene repeatedly in my mind, recalling the startling way our kiss began, and then how I'd allowed it to transform into something I wanted—something I needed.

Regret hit my empty stomach.

My hands rubbed at my eyes, and I ran a hand through my loose, wavy hair. I groaned and sat up in bed, draping my head over my knees. I shouldn't have allowed the kiss to happen. It didn't mean anything. I knew Shane wouldn't think twice about it, and I wondered if I should feel used.

But I had used him, too. Maddie's death lingered over me like a rain cloud, every day threatening to pour down the accompanying guilt and despair linked with her memories. I'd enjoyed the temporary amnesia from constantly thinking about her. I supposed that made Shane and me even. We both got what we wanted, and we could move on.

My cell phone chirped, signaling a text message. It was from Shane and read, "*Good morning, beautiful. Do*

I get to see you today?"

Wait, what?

I read the text one more time, confusion hitting my eyebrows. What happened to the one-night stand idea? Not that I liked the idea, but it was certainly easier than… whatever Shane's text implied.

In less than thirty minutes, I was dressed in warm running gear, an iPod attached to my arm and headphones dangling loosely around my neck.

"Allie, are you sure you want to run this morning?" Mom asked from the breakfast table. She took a bite of pancakes from the plate she'd put together for me, claiming them after I politely declined. "It's cold out there. Why don't you wait for it to warm up this afternoon?"

I lifted my shoe onto the chair to tie my lime-green shoelaces, a brilliant contrast to the black Asics encasing my feet. "It's just one of those mornings," I said, the line I always used if I'd had a Maddie-related nightmare or a case of insomnia. Mom knew that running cleared my head and often helped me sleep better at night. She never questioned me once I released my key phrase. I felt bad for lying this time, but I didn't feel like hashing out boy issues with her right now. I would figure it out.

My feet hit the pavement, thumping in steady repetition. The chilly November air folded me in its embrace and I fought against it, my muscles fighting to warm up and push through the cold. Saturday mornings were often peaceful at this time. Cars that normally sped by on the way to work rested quietly in their garages.

Doors and windows remained shut while families enjoyed their day off together. I passed a few people walking their dogs, a few joggers… I returned a friendly nod and kept running. Eyes didn't follow me, wondering if I was ok or pausing to judge my behavior. I didn't have to accept advice or explain how I was feeling. I simply ran until I could hear my heartbeat in my ears and feel my breath inhale and exhale methodically.

Three miles out, I paused to catch my breath, my chest slightly burning from the cold. I wiggled my fingers for warmth and stretched my tight hamstring. A car pulled up alongside the road with the window rolled down. Tara called out to me.

"Good morning, crazy girl!"

I walked over to the window and peered inside. Resting my hands on the window frame, my fingers appreciated the flow of heat from the vents. I needed to start wearing gloves. "Hi, Tara. What are you doing here?"

"I stopped by and your mom told me your route, so I thought I'd pick you up for breakfast. We need to talk!" Her eyes lit up with excitement, and she smiled knowingly.

I groaned. "What is it you think we need to talk about?"

"Oh, stop it already. I know about you and Shane. Come on, get in here! Let's grab some breakfast."

Hesitation and annoyance dragged my movement, but I relented. It was better that I explained the situation to her than allow Tara to spread faulty news. There was enough of that going on already. Stepping into the car, the radio blared the latest hits. I took a final glance at the peaceful, empty sidewalk with longing.

We drove to a café just down the block. Tara sipped on hot chocolate while I wrapped my hands around a mug of herbal tea. Blueberry muffins sat between us on our small, round table for two.

"What do you mean—you're confused?" Tara asked, leaning towards me. "This is awesome! Me and Austin—you and Shane. It doesn't get any cooler than best friends dating best friends!"

"So you've said," I murmured, picking at the streusel on my muffin. This whole thing started because of that ridiculous notion of hers. I rubbed the grains of sugar between my fingers. "Shane's hot and everything, but I'm not sure there's more to our relationship than that." I reflected on the fumbled conversations we'd had so far, none of which were inspiring, or comforting in the least.

Tara put her muffin down from her mouth. "Well, don't you think there *could* be? You've only hung out a couple of times."

"I don't know," I said, "But right now, he's a temporary distraction and I'm content to leave it at that."

Tara tapped her finger on the table as though stifling impatience. "That's not how he describes it from his end." She held out her iPhone, scrolling through text messages between her and Austin. Some of them were texts between Shane and Austin that had made their way to Tara.

One text from Shane in particular caught my eye. *"I don't know, man. There's something about her that I really like. She's a little tough to crack, but I'm up for the challenge."*

I didn't know if I should feel flattered or irritated at being perceived and discussed as a "challenge." And didn't the term "crack" suggest I was a nut?

"The point is," Tara interrupted, "he likes you, and I really think you two could hit it off."

"Why do you care so much?" I asked, not hiding the annoyance in my tone.

"Because Allie, it's been fun going out on dates and to parties with you. It almost feels like it used to be, you know... before." Tara dropped her lashes momentarily, rubbing her lips together with uncertainty. She glanced back up at me, probably wondering if I caught her meaning. Of course I did. All anyone wanted was for me to go "back to normal," so they could cross me off their list of worries and return to *their* normal life, too.

I stood up, wrapping a napkin around my muffin and unintentionally molding my grip into it. "Let's just get out of here, ok? Thanks for buying breakfast." Before I could stalk out the door, Tara grabbed my wrist, standing so her eyes met mine.

"Look, I'm sorry, ok? I know your cousin's death still affects you. I'm your best friend—I understand how you feel." I fidgeted at her last statement, but she carried on unaware. "Allie, I'm not trying to be rude, but at some point, don't you think it's time to move on? You can't let Maddie's death hold you prisoner. She wouldn't want that for you."

I didn't like her speaking for Maddie, like she knew her. Tara knew next to nothing about her. My eyes brimmed without my consent. I swallowed hard, hoping to somehow drain the tears before they spilled over. "Tara… don't you think that if I could forget about Maddie's death, I would? Do you really think I'm choosing to feel this way?" If I'd learned anything so far, it was that grief didn't have a switch to conveniently turn on and off. On the contrary, sometimes it felt like grief flew on autopilot, navigating my emotions against my will.

Tara wrapped her arms around me momentarily. She faced me again with her hands on my shoulders. Her olive-green eyes glistened just a bit. "Maybe it's time you at least *talked* about it. Nobody knows exactly what happened out there but you. That's why all those stupid rumors are going around. People probably wouldn't care so much, except that you're being so secretive about the whole thing that it peaks their interest." She grabbed one of my hands. "I'm your *best* friend and even I don't know what happened. She just fell in… right?"

I fell back into my chair, glancing out the window. "No good will come from me rehashing that day—trust me." My mouth tightened, teeth clenched.

Tara put up her hands with a shake of her head. "Ok, fine. I get it. Keep it to yourself if you think that's best. But I just hate to see everything you've worked for at this point in high school get kicked to the curb. We could have *a lot* of fun this year." She peered at me earnestly. "It's your senior year. It'll be gone before you know it."

I stared back at her. "Is this why you brought up Shane today? You want me to embrace senior year by pretending to like him?"

Tara shifted her stance. "Not 'pretend' necessarily. But give him a chance. I think it'd be helpful for you to have something else to think about."

While I could agree that the distraction with Shane over the last week had been refreshing, I didn't know how helpful it could be in the long run. I told Tara I'd consider it and asked her to let it be for now.

When she dropped me off at my doorstep, I didn't return with the clear head I'd hoped for. I frowned at the Lexus parked in my driveway. Someone quite wealthy was visiting my house—or at least the *son* of someone quite wealthy. With anticipation, I stepped into the house.

Shane sat on my couch, chatting comfortably with Mom, while Leah and Taylor peeked at him from the hallway. I glared at the two of them, and they smothered giggles. Shane and Mom turned my way.

"Hi, honey! Your friend stopped by…" She raised her eyebrows at me and failed to contain a teasing smile.

Oh, come on... Her, too? I knew she would love nothing more than to believe I was hanging out with friends and even dating again. Maybe she was the one planting ideas in Tara's head.

I met Shane's penetrating gaze. Despite the annoyance at myself for kissing him, I couldn't help the instantaneous butterflies in my stomach. Some of my confusion flew out the window as a magnet of attraction drew me towards him. I couldn't help but like the way he was checking me out, even with Mom present. There was an arrogance about him that both repelled and lured me. Tightening my tousled ponytail, I asked, "Shane, what are you doing here?"

He stood up and closed the gap between us. Mom also rose to her feet, watching us carefully as if she were trying to clue in on the status of our relationship.

Good luck with that.

"You never responded to my text," Shane said. "So I figured that meant you wouldn't mind if I stopped by."

"That was your conclusion, huh?" I folded my arms but released a half-smile, realizing I didn't entirely mind him being there. It was easier to write him off when he wasn't standing in my presence—especially with his cologne baiting me.

"I thought we could team up and sell raffle tickets together this afternoon," Shane suggested.

Raffle tickets… I'd forgotten we needed to go door to door in support of our basketball fundraiser. "Uh, sure, if that's how you want to spend your Saturday," I said.

Shane puffed out his chest, deepening his voice for effect. "Well, you know, with our powers combined…"

"Our powers being?"

Shane smirked. "Well, obviously, I have all the charm. We just need to hope *women* open the door." Noticing my jaw drop in disgust, he added, "And you have all the wit!" When I still appeared less than impressed by his chauvinistic sales pitch, he continued, "My looks will lure them in, and you can hook them with an intelligent, convincing speech about our basketball teams' need for cash. The girls' team was all the rage last year at Sectionals, so your part shouldn't be hard."

I scoffed at him. "When you put it that way, I have the know-how *and* the reputation. Sounds like you need me more than I need you. That's why you really came by, isn't it?"

Shane took a step closer. He lowered his voice, his fingers lightly touching my hand. "What do *you* think?" He paused to briefly trace his finger along the back of my hand. "You don't really think I forgot about last night so easily, did you?"

I swallowed, my nerves dancing inside me. I cast my eyes in search of Mom, but she, thankfully, had already stepped out of the room—probably to chase away my spying sisters, who were also nowhere to be seen.

I had a decision to make, and only moments to do it. Everything about my response would determine where Shane and I were headed. The question remained—to acquiesce or shut him down? The natural chemistry between us grew every time I saw him. There was no doubt about that. Perhaps I'd discover more depth to his personality, like Tara said. Or maybe I could just go through the motions long enough to thwart everyone's ongoing assessment of me.

My lashes slowly drew upwards to meet Shane's striking features. Placing a tentative hand on his arm, I smiled.

"Of course not. And I'd love to go with you."

CHAPTER SEVEN

"You can't drive us around to sell raffle tickets in your Lexus," I said with a laugh. As planned, Shane had arrived mid-afternoon so we could earn money for basketball. "No one will believe we're in need. Come on, I'll drive."

We spent the afternoon meandering through different neighborhoods, getting in and out of the car and knocking on doors. By the time evening greeted us, we were cold and worn out but pleased with our results.

"We should celebrate." Shane indicated the clipboard containing the list of names from our raffle ticket buyers. "You hungry?"

"I might be," I said, "Depending on the place. What's on the menu?"

"Ever been to Hank's?"

"Nope."

"Come on then. You won't be disappointed."

"What makes you so sure?" I asked. "We hardly know each other. I could have very picky dietary needs." I withheld my laugh, baiting his confidence.

Shane didn't appear the least bit worried, but he asked, "You're not a vegetarian, are you?"

I shook my head. "But if I were, would that be a problem?"

"No, not at all. Actually, I was hoping you were. I was looking forward to the challenge of convincing you otherwise. Once you eat at Hank's, there's no turning back."

Shane's directions led us to an old food truck, its exterior weathered and grey. My surprise must have escaped me because Shane smiled and said, "What? Just because I drive a Lexus, I can't appreciate food trucks?"

"I didn't say anything about you and your Lexus. Although, since you brought it up, why in the world does your dad let you drive his car?"

"He trusts me. I haven't even had as much as a fender bender." Shane shrugged. "Besides, I can be very… persuasive… when I want to be. I tend to get what I want."

I couldn't help but blush at the way he was looking at me, clearly referencing more than his dad's car. I decided to move our conversation elsewhere. "Speaking of your dad, I was wondering… just how Italian are you?"

"I see you've been doing some research on me," Shane said. "What else did you discover about me?"

I let out a laugh. "Yeah, you wish. It's pretty simple, really. Your last name is 'Moretti. That screams Italian all by itself—that, and it's November, which means everyone else is jealous of your never-ending summer tan." I pulled up the sleeve of my shirt for emphasis. My previously golden skin from months in the sun had long since disappeared, whereas Shane still held onto his mildly olive skin tone.

Shane nodded, and I noticed his strong profile. "Ok, you've discovered my not-so-subtle secret. My grandpa is full Italian, making me only a quarter." He straightened his posture with a boastful grin. "I'd say it works for me though." He let out a laugh so I knew his arrogance was in jest, but I couldn't disagree with him. His dark features and warm undertones made it hard to look away… except for when he caught me staring.

Exiting the car, the smell of grilled meat teased my senses, making my mouth water and my stomach growl. At last, our food was delivered in our hands, packaged in butcher paper. We opted to sit in my car with the heat blasting to warm up from standing in line outside.

"All right," I said, removing the fully loaded wrap from its packaging. "Just know that I am judging you with every bite." Shane laughed, but didn't backpedal on his promise that I would love it. I'd trusted him to order for me. I sank my teeth into the bursting tortilla, the juices from the grilled chicken and steak blending deliciously with a sweet and spicy BBQ sauce. I closed my eyes with a laugh. "Oh wow… this is amazing…."

Shane watched me take another bite, not the least bit surprised by my response. "And you doubted me…" His eyes paused on my mouth, and I instantly became very self-conscious of eating in front of him.

I quickly swallowed, using the back of my hand to swipe at a smear of BBQ on my lips. "Ok, this is not fair. You can't just sit there and watch me eat. You make me nervous!" Even as I spoke, juice from the bottom of the wrap started leaking, dripping onto my jeans. I titled the wrap, scrambling to smooth the butcher paper across my lap. Juice continued to dribble down my hand and trailed along my wrist. "You lose points because they didn't give us napkins." I scowled at him when he laughed at me, eying the mess falling onto my lap.

"Why do I make you nervous?" Shane asked, his eyes still roaming my face, bouncing from my eyes to my lips again. "You have napkins right there, by the way." He leaned in, reaching over me towards the side of my door. He grabbed a handful of leftover napkins from a previous fast food stop. His body lingered against mine a moment longer than necessary before he handed one to me. "You got a little something… everywhere," he teased with a smirk. I smacked his face with the napkin.

"Ok, I never professed to have strong etiquette. Here, hold this." I handed him my wrap, which was now bundled with the extra napkins. I licked juice from my fingers, forcing a laugh. "Yes, very attractive, I know…" I hoped making a joke would disguise my embarrassment. My eyes flicked over to Shane's amused expression.

"Very attractive," he agreed. Then he added, "You are, actually."

I bit my lip, inhaling deeply to chase away whatever was twirling in my stomach. Crumpling the dirty napkins, I shoved them into the cup holders of the console. "Ok, just… give me that." I snatched back my wrap with a shy smile. "I bet you're glad you didn't drive us in your Lexus now."

"Yeah, no kidding, right?"

"Whatever. Go on; let's see how well you do then."

"You don't mess with experts, Allie." He pulled the wrapper off his food, peeling from the top but leaving the butcher paper wrapping attached at the bottom. He took a huge bite, cleanly filling his mouth. Once he managed to swallow, he made a show of dabbing at the corner of his mouth with his napkin. He grinned. "And that's how it's done."

Following my food fiasco in the car, Austin called, inviting us to meet up with him and a couple of friends. Tara was at his place, too. Shane didn't even bother knocking before he opened Austin's front door. I guess being best friends since sixth grade allowed for that kind of behavior. We stepped inside.

"Good, you made it." Austin hustled towards us and threw some clothes at Shane. "Here, put these on."

Shane caught the pants. They looked like army fatigues, dark in color with printed camouflage. Shane's eyes lit up, like he understood where this was going.

"What's that for?" I asked, noticing Austin wearing the same type of pants and a black hoodie. Tara stepped out of the bathroom down the hall. She wore tight, dark denim pants and a forest green shirt that said ARMY across the front. What stood out the most was the pink bandana running across her forehead.

"You're here! This is for you." She handed me an identical pink bandana with black swirls patterned on it. "How'd it go selling raffles?"

I accepted the bandana in confusion. "It was good… Ok, what's with the outfit?"

Tara laughed. "Don't be jealous because I'm rockin' the pink bandana. I might need to try this look at school…"

I shook my head. "Please don't."

"I think she looks sexy," Austin said, kissing her cheek as he walked past her.

"Thanks, baby," Tara said, watching her boyfriend walk down the hall. Two guys emerged from a bedroom, both shorter in stature. The guy with light brown hair wore jeans, as well as a green hoodie with the word ARMY printed in black letters across the chest. Tara introduced him as Ben. His redheaded friend, Landon, was dressed in similar style. I vaguely recognized him from the wrestling team.

I remembered now that Austin's oldest brother served in the army for a time, which explained the explosion of camouflage in tonight's attire—but I had yet to discover the purpose. The pink bandana had to be Tara's own personal touch, of course. I eyed the girly material with disdain.

"Oh, just put it on," Tara said, folding it for me.

"There are a couple of more shirts in the closet if you want them."

"Shane?" I asked, my expression begging for clarification.

"We're going to the golf course," Shane said with nonchalance, though excitement failed to hide behind his expression. "Remember how I told you we hang out there sometimes?"

I remembered his comment about getting creative. "I take it we're not golfing…"

"Nope, not quite."

Landon pulled his hoodie over his buzzed head. "Let's do this."

Before long, we parked on the street just outside the golf course.

"Sorry it's kind of cold, but you'll warm up soon," Shane said to me as we hopped out of my car. "Oh, be right back." He slipped over to the trunk of Austin's car, where our friends were applying a couple of more layers, and he came back with a pair of leather gloves.

"Thanks." I slipped one on. They were too big but still warm. I pulled the right glove over my fingers and noticed Shane's full name embroidered along the wrist in cursive. I gave Shane a sideways glance. "You embroidered them with your name? Are you for real?" Hearing my words, Shane's buddies joined in, razzing him about his extra special "lady gloves".

Shane swiftly punched his friends in the chest. "Bunch of idiots… You know why I have those!" Their laughter carried through the still air. To me, he said, "My mom gave them to me last Christmas, ok? Why do you think they stay buried in Austin's trunk?"

I snickered lightly. "Ok, fair enough."

"All right, enough of this." Shane pulled a black beanie low over his forehead, emphasizing his dark eyes. He put his hands on my shoulders and turned me around. Giving me a light push, he said, "We're hoofing it from here. Let's go."

The six of us cut across the golf course on foot until we reached the outskirts on the opposite side. Austin led the way, suddenly crouching behind a line of bushes. A row of houses lined up next to each other, each one as ornate as the next.

"Open the bags," he ordered, pulling out a slingshot hooked to his hip. Ben and Landon unzipped the backpacks, handing out slingshots and paintballs.

"Who wants the first shot?" Ben asked, his fingers eagerly stretching the sling in his hands.

"I do," Tara said, a devilish grin spreading across her face.

"You?" Landon asked, though I could sense the hint of approval behind his surprise. "All right, here you go." He handed her the slingshot and one blue paintball.

"You're really going to do it?" I whispered. The most I'd ever contributed to vandalism was toilet-papering houses in middle school.

"Why not?" she asked, placing the paintball in the pouch. "I don't want the guys thinking we can't keep up.

It was my idea for us to come." She turned to her target, the unmarked home standing tall and wide. She reared back on the sling shot… and released. The paintball fell short about a foot. The guys quietly groaned. "Hold on, hold on…" Tara muttered. "Give me that." She snatched a green ball and, with determination, pulled harder on the sling. When she let go, the ball sailed in a perfect arch before splattering below the window.

"Got it!"

"That's my girl," Austin said. Tara beamed.

The guys quickly followed suit, grabbing ammo and loading their slings. With rapid fire, the row of houses took one hit after another. I watched, too nervous to participate.

"What are you waiting for? Come on." Austin put the slingshot in my hand. "It's harmless. Washes right off."

I saw Landon peering at me, one eyebrow raised. He blew air through his lips and shook his head before firing another paintball.

Fine. I'll do it. I didn't need anyone labeling me as the weakest link.

I pulled back the sling, stretching as far as it could go. The paintball nailed the side of the house with a splat. I had to admit—there was something satisfying about seeing that small ball of color pop.

We kept moving, not wanting to stay in one location too long. We snuck along the border of the golf course, crouching low when lights sprang on, and giggling softly when we heard the uproar from upset homeowners. Ben warned us we'd need to call it quits soon before anyone spotted us.

For our final target, Shane led us to the runoff ditch bordering the golf course. We lay on our stomachs, eyeing the gleaming white house directly across the way. Not only was the house white, but there was an expensive white truck parked right in front.

"Ohh, this house…" Landon said, his eyes taking on a hypnotic gaze, "is just begging to be hammered."

"It's beautiful…" Ben's expression matched Landon's, as though they couldn't help but be drawn to this perfectly white, last target—our final attack.

Landon revealed the last of our paintball supply. We were running low, but there was just enough for a few more shots each. We kneeled on the ground, slingshots loaded, and then we let the paintballs fly. The air between us filled with snickers and playful banter. I shouldn't have been enjoying myself as much as I was. I knew Mom would kill me for defacing homes… but it felt so good to laugh again, and to let go of behaving how I *should*.

Knowing these were my last shots, I wanted to make them count—just in case the moral part of me decided not to do this again. My fingers were hot inside Shane's leather gloves, and they were too big anyway, hindering my grip on the slingshot. I slipped it off and flexed my fingers.

I elbowed Shane. "Watch this." Eager to show my improvement, I pulled back as hard as I could and then let go.

"Nice shot, rookie," Shane said, nodding with his lips pushed out. "Imagine how good you'll be next time." I decided not to think about whether there would be a next time or not.

"I have the last shot," Austin claimed, his fingers folding over the final red paintball. We surveyed the house and truck, both now decorated in colorful polka dots. "Front door in three… two…"

"No, wait!" Ben hissed.

Too late.

The front door opened just as Austin's finger's released the small, leather strap. "One." The paintball hit the middle-aged man who opened the door, straight at his burly chest.

Tara and I gasped. The guys swore, scrambling to gather the gear. It was then that I noticed the shotgun in the man's arms. We didn't wait to see if he'd already cocked it.

"Move, move, move!" Landon urged.

We tore away from our hiding spot, hearing the man bellowing after us. "You freaking kids!"

"Oh, man, we are in so much trouble." I stayed close behind Shane.

He didn't turn his head but called back, "No, we're not. We're only in trouble if we get caught."

"Yeah," Austin agreed from the front. "It's not like this is the first time we've had to run. Keep movin'!" He put a hand on Tara's back, keeping her in front of him.

We crossed onto the green. My body moved fast, warm inside my layers—all except the fingers on my right hand, which I opened and closed to keep the blood circulating…

I almost tripped as I came to a halt. Realization hit my gut. "Shane! Your glove!"

"What'd you say?" Shane paused from running. He called out to me in a hushed voice. "Come on, Allie, we can't stand around. He might have called the cops."

My face flushed with heat. "No, no! Your glove, with your name embroidered on it. I dropped it on the ground!"

"You what?" Shane moved towards me, his eyes widening. He let out a breath and then smoothed his concerned expression before looking back at our friends. Tara had skittered to a stop, ignoring Austin's hand on her.

"What's up, Allie?" Her pink bandana had fallen from her head, now twisted in one fist.

"Just go," Shane said to the group. "We need to double back and grab something. We have Allie's car. Meet back at my place!"

Shane and I ran back the way we came, sticking close to the trees. "I'm really sorry," I said between breaths.

"Don't worry about it," Shane breathed. "It's better if we split up anyway. Besides, I'm sure the guy's just really pissed, but he's not going to find us." After another minute, we approached our previous spot. "Stay low," Shane warned. We peeked out towards the white house speckled with evidence of our delinquency. There was no sign of the man. Or the truck.

"Uh oh…" I said. "Where's the—"

Before I finished speaking, we heard angry gears grinding in the distance. I inhaled, looking to Shane, my heart thumping and preparing to flee. Shane swallowed, and then let his natural confidence wash over him. "If he's in his truck, we're fine. He can't come onto the golf course with his truck." We searched the ground.

There. I picked up the missing glove, pulling it over my fingers. I smiled at Shane in relief, glad that I hadn't totally butchered the evening. We quickened our pace to return to the green, knowing we'd have to move fast across the fairway.

An engine roared in the distance, coming fast. We looked to our right, catching sight of the headlights careening across the bridge.

"No way…" Shane grabbed my arm to stop me. We both saw the truck approaching *on the golf course,* leaving the golf cart bridge and moving towards the green. Since we were still on the edge, he hadn't seen us yet, but he was headed our way.

"Back to the ditch," Shane said.

I followed him, trusting that he knew his way around and would get us out of this mess. Back at our original hideout, we jumped into the ditch and then climbed up onto the road. The once "perfectly white" house stood beside us. We took off down the street.

"Let's get far enough away from here," Shane

huffed, "and then I'll call Austin to come pick us up." I nodded.

It was a good plan—but we didn't get far.

Police sirens whined in the distance, nearing our location. It took only a few moments to realize we were running towards them, sharing the same road. But to turn back, we knew the man in the truck could return to his house any minute, or perhaps he was still roaming the golf course. We could only assume the police were coming for us, which maybe wasn't a bad thing considering the guy in the truck had a shotgun. Still, neither option, police nor the madman, would end with promising results. We paused, hesitating for a moment, eying the approaching lights. We didn't need to discuss the repercussions of vandalism.

"We gotta get back onto the course!" I said to Shane, my breaths heaving in and out almost in sync with his. We clamored back into the ditch and ran towards the green once more, praying the man in the truck had returned to the road to meet the cops at his home.

No such luck.

Headlights caught us in a brilliant spotlight, though the truck seemed to be two hundred feet away still. It seemed he'd been hiding out, waiting to spot us. Seconds later, rotating red and blue lights were on the street behind us. A huge spotlight caught us in its crossfire. We were surrounded.

"Put your hands where we can see them!" An officer's voiced carried through his megaphone from his position on the street.

My body trembled, exhaustion and fear working against me. "Shane..." I murmured. I raised my hands into the air.

The officer's voice boomed into the megaphone again. "You in the truck! This is Officer Newman. Turn off your headlights!"

"They can't see us... They're blinding each other—they can't see us!" Shane pulled me after him to the left. "The trees—get to the trees!" We ran twenty feet before diving into the bushes. I felt my clothing snag and was grateful for my long sleeves.

The man in the truck cut his headlights, leaving the one giant spotlight illuminating an empty spot of grass. Both Shane and I tried to quiet our breathing while we peered out from our new position.

"They're going to come over here," I whispered, fear threatening to take over.

"Don't move."

In the next moment, the spotlight swung towards us again. Before I could even think of what to do, Shane threw his body on top of mine, his chest lying flat on my back. I exhaled a puff of air from his sudden weight. The light roved around us, swinging ominously back and forth, seeking us out. Understanding swept over me. Shane's camouflaged attire would help us blend into the brush, shielding us.

The spotlight surveying the hill of trees continued for one very long minute. Adrenaline raced through me, in part from the chase but also because of Shane's body on top of mine. The side of his face pressed against my left cheek, our lips close. I thought I could feel his heart pumping straight into my back, his body pinning me to the ground.

Finally, the spotlight lifted, though the police cars remained in position. Shane turned his face even more towards mine. "Allie," he spoke softly.

"Hmm?" was all I could murmur, my face growing warm in anticipation of his kiss. Shane paused, a breath away, his lips mischievously close to mine. He whispered again.

"We need to get out of here." He slid his body from mine. I lay there, confused, for a moment longer. I took an easier breath, exhaling a mix of emotions, although I thought I caught Shane smile as he crouched next to me. "They might come after us on foot. Come on, stay low."

I mimicked Shane's curved back, keeping my head bowed as I watched him lead the way up the hill of trees. Part of me wanted to shove him to the ground for messing with me—not that I could prove he was playing games. Shane did, in fact, save me from getting caught by the police and a gun-wielding maniac. Legitimately, this was not a good time to hang out and kiss each other. Still, he'd been teasing me and he liked it. I frowned at his back, still trying to figure out how I felt about him.

Shane turned to me as we trudged up the hill. "Not a bad night, huh?" he said, adjusting his beanie low over his eyes. Even though I was winded, I could still feel adrenaline pumping through my body, keeping me alert. I removed my bandana from my forehead, wondering about Tara and the others.

"Are your Saturday nights always this crazy?" I asked. Swiping the bandana along my cheek, I attempted to wipe dirt off my face.

"Nah…" He paused with a smile. "Only when rookies come along."

I smacked his shoulder. "I said I was sorry! Come on, I did pretty well otherwise, right?"

Shane chuckled. "Yeah, you did all right." Shane pointed across the golf course. "Look, there's your car. We're nearly there."

We picked up the pace, eager to put the evening behind us.

CHAPTER EIGHT

There it was again.

This time, there was no mistaking the dirty look thrown my way from the girl with jet-black hair, seated a couple of tables away. She wasn't even trying to hide it this time. The dark eye makeup drawn around her eyes emphasized the scowl. She had one thin leg crossed over the other while her left arm draped across her stomach. The fingers of her right hand played with her silver earrings, the loose chain decorating the entire curve of her cartilage.

I nudged Tara beside me. "Do you know that girl? Why does it look like she's trying to strangle me with her eyes?"

Tara munched on a chip before glancing across the cafeteria. "Oh, the girl with the bad dye-job?" Tara's observation was accurate. The girl's hair was so unnaturally black that it washed out her already pale skin. "Not sure, but if she keeps it up, I'll gladly go find out." With both Tara and I returning her stare, the girl finally turned away to mutter something to her friend. No doubt, the words were about us, since the equally skinny friend sent a look of disgust our way.

"All right, what's her problem?" I was used to people talking about me out of curiosity or pity, but not with such blatant dislike.

"She's just jealous." Taylor's voice spoke from behind me. She and Leah placed their trays on our table. "That's Crystal Jennings. She's a sophomore and already notorious for hooking up with all the hot juniors and seniors."

"I'm pretty sure your boyfriend was near the top of her list," Leah added. She sat down. "Crystal takes pride in completing her checklist. At least, she'd proved that last year as a highly confident freshman."

I felt the need to clarify. "Ok, first of all, Shane's not my boyfriend."

"Isn't he?" Tara asked.

"I hooked up with him one night and was almost arrested the next. I'm not sure that qualifies him as becoming my boyfriend." While I'd kissed a couple of guys in the past, and had a boyfriend for a short time, I'd never let any relationship get serious. It was unchartered territory as far as I was concerned, and I wasn't sure I wanted to explore it with Shane.

"Well," Tara said, "Here he comes with *my* boyfriend, so maybe you can clear that up with Shane right now." She waved at Austin's and Shane's approaching figures. They both sauntered across the cafeteria floor, only moments away from reaching us.

"Tara, no!" I hissed. "I am not having that conversation here in the cafeteria, especially with that creepy girl staring me down." Shane had flirted with me all day Saturday, and he'd had the opportunity to kiss me at the golf course but hadn't taken it. He'd teased me instead. Not that kissing made him my boyfriend… but maybe he had decided a one-night stand was good enough after all. That was what I'd wanted in the first place so maybe it put us on the same page again.

"Relax. I'm just kidding," she muttered, her teasing grin transforming into a full smile. She stood, and Austin embraced her with strong arms before kissing her cheek. They seemed natural together—nothing forced or uncomfortable about their interaction.

And then there was Shane and I. We'd had fun together on Saturday, but I felt unsure about his intentions with me. Or even my intentions with him.

I didn't know what to do with myself, as I stared up at Shane from my seated position. His brown eyes met mine. "Hey, Shane." Was I supposed to hug him? He didn't make a move, so I didn't either. Instead, his smooth expression greeted me with a simple smile—a smile that set my nerves dancing on edge despite myself.

"What's up, Allie?" Shane appeared so at ease in his skin, like nothing could rattle him.

"Oh, not much," I managed to say. A sense of shyness crept over me. I felt more comfortable when it was just the two of us, rather than having to worry about spectators. It didn't help that I could feel the dark-haired Crystal observing and assessing our interaction. She was probably wondering if it was safe to make her move with

Shane in the near future—which, considering I could think of nothing interesting to say in the moment, could very well be soon.

"So…" Leah said, breaking the awkward silence. "Did you guys hear Walsh is out for the season?"

"No way!" Tara said. She pulled away from Austin, fully engaging in the conversation. "What happened?"

Leah led the conversation about Maya Walsh, the critical point guard for one of our rivals and how her broken ankle would need surgery. Apparently bored with our conversation, Shane and Austin wandered off to the lunch line. With a subtle move, I squeezed Leah's knee in thanks for saving my inability to speak.

Still, I peeked at Shane, thinking about Saturday night. After we had reached my car, we regrouped with our friends and things remained casual between us. We shared our escape stories, which proved less harrowing for our friends than for Shane and me. Shane and I laughed about how we'd flung ourselves into the trees and away from the police spotlight. Shane didn't mention how he and his camouflaged self had fallen on top of me, so I didn't either. He also hadn't tried to kiss me when our night was over, and I couldn't figure out if I was more relieved or disappointed.

By the time Shane and Austin returned to our table with their food, my social skills had warmed up enough to chat about my lazy Sunday and the monotony of school life… It wasn't until the bell rang and our group broke away for classes that Shane pulled me aside. His fingers lightly touched my elbow to hold me back.

"What's going on?" I asked.

"Nothing. Just wondering if you're ok. You seem a little… uncomfortable today."

I hated that my cheeks turned pink, proving him right. I wished I could read him as well as he could read me. "I'm not… ok, maybe a little. I don't know…"

Shane grinned. "You're pretty cute when you're nervous."

Ah! Flirting again! And all I could do was blush and feel tongue-tied. Why did he wait until we were alone to talk like this? I couldn't play his games. I flicked my gaze around the emptying cafeteria, looking for an exit point—namely Tara or my sisters to chase after. No such luck. I returned Shane's steady gaze. "I'm just getting used to hanging out with people again, I guess." Lame. But it was a truthful statement.

"I can understand that. You *have* kept to yourself a lot this year."

At least he had noticed. It reminded me of the short conversation we'd had at his party when he'd referred to me as a "hermit". I hadn't appreciated it at the time, though it was accurate. When the school year begun, I did whatever I could to be invisible, whether it was hiding in the bathroom stalls, the library, or simply hurrying home right after school to escape social settings. It was too hard knowing how to respond to questions about the accident, or Maddie, and not knowing how much people knew or cared.

"So, how about coming out with us again tonight?" Shane continued.

"It's Monday..."

"Yes..." Shane nodded once. "This is true." The corners of his mouth turned up ever so slightly. He lowered his voice, moving his mouth closer to my ear. "It *is* ok to have a social life beyond the weekend."

An uncomfortable laugh escaped my mouth. I busied myself with tucking hair behind my right ear and licked my lips. I lifted my face to Shane again. "Ok, sure. What's the plan?"

"I'm not sure there is one yet," Shane said, walking with me towards the cafeteria doors. "But it beats doing homework. We'll think of something."

Shane and I drove through a newly developed neighborhood, evident by the freshly painted condos lined up in cookie-cutter fashion. Light peeked through some of the windows, but the further we went, there seemed to be more uninhabited condos.

"Keep going?" Shane asked, speaking into his cell phone to Austin. The neighborhood darkened, quiet and void of people. However, lampposts in the distance provided enough light to see a number of condos currently under construction. "Yeah, I see your car now." Shane hung up the phone. We pulled alongside Austin's car, which was parked inconspicuously behind a high retaining wall.

"What are we doing here?" I asked, peeking out the window. Then I saw the shadowed outlines of our friends. They were sitting on the scaffolding of an unfinished condo across from us.

Shane grabbed my hand and pulled me after him. Reaching the bottom of the scaffolding, we received a chorus of greetings.

"Allie!" Tara stood up and leaned over the metal railing. "Where've you guys been?" She received an arm nudge from Ben.

"Yo, quiet down," he said. "We don't need anyone calling the cops on us."

"Yeah, we had enough of that already," Shane said, nudging my arm. I smiled, though I checked out my surroundings, wondering why we'd need to worry about cops again. I followed Shane up the ladder, joining our friends on the second floor of the scaffolding. Landon threw Shane a can of beer, and then held one towards me in question. Oh. Now I understood.

"No, I'm good." I shoved my hands in my coat pocket, watching Shane pop the can open without hesitation. He took a swig.

"Come on," he said, motioning for me to sit along the edge. I sat down beside him with Tara on my right. She leaned over and linked arms with me.

"Thanks for coming. How long do you think we can get away with 'studying at each other's house' before our moms figure it out?"

"Mm... I'm pretty sure *my* mom knows we're just hanging out and not doing anything productive." While I hadn't shared details with Mom, she still seemed pretty excited that I had a social life again. Tonight, she eyed me a moment longer than necessary when I said I was going over to Tara's to study, even though that wasn't out of the norm for us. Tara and I both cared about our grades. Mom didn't question me though. Still, even having her silent consent, I felt a little guilty. She would not approve if she knew drinking was involved. Tara's eyes followed mine.

"It'll be fine," she whispered.

With boys dominating our little group, Tara and I found ourselves listening to them tell war stories about weekend pranks they had pulled throughout their high school careers. We shared laughs, picturing the dumb stunts they'd pulled, including Shane partially falling through the roof of an old shack. There had been no reason to climb onto the decrepit roof they'd discovered while camping one weekend. Their way of thinking rolled more along the lines of, "Why not?" By the end of the hour, I found myself relaxing and having a good time, my feet dangling over the edge of the platform.

Shane put one arm around my shoulders, pulling me closer. "You warm enough?" he asked.

"Yeah, I'm fine." I tried to hide my shivers. Shane drew me towards him, close enough for his body heat to seep into mine.

"I'm going up," Landon announced, carrying

another can of beer to the far side of the scaffolding. Teetering just slightly, he steadied himself as he prepared to climb the rungs. "You guys coming?"

"Hey, be careful!" I said, looking to Shane for support. Landon rolled his eyes, while Shane only chuckled.

"Don't worry about him," Shane said to me. "He's just buzzed." He studied my face for a moment. I didn't return his smile, keeping my eyes on Landon instead. Soon, his body disappeared onto the next floor. I heard his footsteps above us.

"Heeyyy, check it out!" Landon's voice called. It sounded like he was inside the house. One by one, the rest of the group climbed the scaffolding to join him. I trailed after them, reaching the top scaffolding and then slipping through a window onto the third story of the condo. We found Landon inside what appeared to be the master bedroom. Just beyond the main room was an open wall that led onto a spacious balcony.

"How tight would that be to have hot tub out here right now?" Austin said.

"Not a bad view, either." Tara stood at the edge of the balcony, peering out at the dim neighborhood. Just down the road, headlights warned of an approaching vehicle.

"Get down!" Ben said. We ducked and slipped back into the house, hiding within the unfinished walls.

I peeked out the window. "It's gone, I think."

"I don't like how that car was creepin'," Ben said.

"Someone might have spotted us earlier. Come on, grab your beer." Everyone else headed towards the window to exit onto the scaffolding the way we entered.

Intrigued by the interior, I said, "I just want to explore the rooms real quick. I'll take the stairs and see you out front."

Shane grabbed my hand. "I better come with you in case you fall or something." He took another sip of beer. My brows knitted together and I removed the can from his hand, placing it on a windowsill.

"Hey—"

I interrupted his protest. "If anyone's going to fall, it certainly won't be me." Shane let out a humored sound, but followed me down the steps.

"At least my shoes don't echo throughout the entire house," he countered, eying my slightly heeled boots that were clopping loudly with each step.

"Ok, I'll give you that one…"

We poked around the different rooms, trying to imagine what each might be when completed. I made my way to the front entrance, peering through the empty frame where the door should be. "I kinda like this place. Although I'm really not a fan of—" I stopped, hearing our friends scrambling on the scaffolding above us. Shane grabbed my shoulders, yanking me inside the house. He pulled me around the corner of the doorframe.

At my objection, he placed a hand over my mouth. It was then that I heard a car slowing down just outside. Shane's eyes warned me to be quiet, both of us knowing it might be that same car again. Someone was, without a doubt, looking for us.

Eying the exit points—which was either the front entrance or bolting to the back door adjacent to the kitchen—I prepared to flee. But after a few moments, the sound of the car faded in the distance. I breathed a sigh of relief.

"You're not very good at this stealth stuff, are you?" Shane teased. "First your shoes… and then you stuck your head out the front door!"

"In my defense, having to constantly stay on guard is new territory for me! Besides, it was only for a second..." My words cut off as Shane placed both of his hands against the wall behind me, leaning in. His mouth met mine, eager and more forceful than our first kiss. I recoiled slightly, the taste of beer distracting. I pushed against his shoulder, though not enough to derail his efforts. My hand slid to his chest instead, feeling the muscle behind his shirt. The scent of his cologne drew me back in.

I closed my eyes, enjoying the moment but also feeling confused inside. I'd wanted him to kiss me again… but was afraid for what it might mean. Would I be able to handle this life with Shane and his rambunctious friends when I was still working through so many emotions? Even in the middle of this kiss, my thoughts turned to Maddie, feeling guilty that I was indulging with Shane and living this life when she was dead. Then again, maybe I didn't want to work through it.

"Shane, what are we doing?" I asked, both of my hands pushing against him until he stopped.

"I think that's fairly obvious," he said, his body still very much in my space.

I let out a quiet sigh. "I like you, Shane. But I'm not sure—"

"We're just having fun, Allie." Shane's quick response surprised me, yet at the same time, I knew I shouldn't be surprised at all. "It's senior year—nothing serious," he continued, one finger slowly tracing the side of my face. "You and I both know this isn't following us into college."

"Oh…" I felt relieved and yet bothered at the same time. I didn't want to worry about the emotional dependence of a relationship, so I was happy he understood that… but something still didn't feel right.

"Does that hurt your feelings?" he asked,

"I… no…" My eyes hit the floorboard, not sure what I was feeling. A part of me liked how I felt being with Shane and feeling attractive—feeling like a normal high school girl again—but I wasn't proud that my motives came from a selfish place of escape. It was easy to forget Maddie and the tough emotions wrapped around her death with Shane around. I knew this solution could only be temporary, but maybe that was what I needed. I could run with it just long enough to keep my head above water, so I wasn't drowning with Maddie all over again.

"Good," Shane said, his hands on my shoulders.

"Because you're a lot of fun when you want to be."

I wasn't entirely sure whether that was a compliment or not, but before I had time to mull it over, our friends came parading down the stairs, laughing about how fast they'd had to climb back into the building.

"That was close!"

"We've got to do this again."

"Hey, give my girl some breathing room!" Tara linked arms with mine and tugged me free from Shane's cornering stance. In a carefree manner, she pulled me out the door towards the cars.

"She's not *your girl* anymore, Tara," Shane called from behind us. At his words, I turned my head to catch him grinning back at me.

Tara laughed as she strutted away with me. "You had a good time, right?" She winked at me, knowing Shane had kissed me again.

"Don't even start, Tara." But I smiled.

CHAPTER NINE

Shane and I didn't make a big announcement about being together, but word spread fast enough. Our interactions weren't as apparent as Tara and Austin's. But maybe people had seen Shane playing with my hair when we sat together at lunch, or noticed the way I smiled more often. Perhaps someone had even seen him pull me into the empty gym a time or two, during the late hours after school when everyone was done with practice—or maybe when Shane, who seemed to enjoy catching me off guard, would pull me into an empty room to kiss me before a teacher walked in. I was getting the sense that he enjoyed the thrill of sneaking around, with or without cops involved.

I thought that by becoming "official" with Shane, I would feel less judged—that all the kids and teachers who had been evaluating me from a distance or whispering about me from the sidelines would cease to exist, or at least diminish in number. Over the next couple of weeks, I found the opposite to be true.

With Shane and I walking hand in hand down the hallways now, not far from Tara and Austin, kids continued to watch me. The difference was, instead of talking about my summer accident and spreading rumors about the details, they seemed to be admiring me for making a comeback. If my story were a sports headline, it might read, *"Against All Odds, Allie Collins Returns!"*

Younger students, especially those in Leah and Taylor's sophomore class, seemed to follow me with admiration—or maybe it was envy. The latter was certainly the case when it came to Crystal. Her dark, smokey-eyed makeup glowered at me, one hand on her narrow hips. I'd often catch her looking me up and down, as if she couldn't figure out why Shane would pick me.

Regardless of the purpose behind people staring, whether it was having Shane's arm linked around my waist or enjoying the stardom at our basketball games, Tara was right—senior year was picking up in pace and becoming exactly what we imagined it could be. It was a refreshing change. I felt like I could hide within my new group of friends—a merger of mine and Tara's friends, and Shane and Austin's. Many of them were athletes, too. I was back where I belonged.

Still, a part of me knew this was all a veneer. Just when I thought I was making strides in getting over last summer's ordeal, images of Maddie drowning would pop into my head—sometimes out of nowhere, and other times, based off harmless comments from others. When kids talked about vacation or swimming, knots would build up in my stomach, or my brain would spiral into headaches that would send me home from school.

I felt pathetic. Weak. I kept telling myself that if I

could pretend to be over Maddie's death, then eventually, those thoughts would seep into my emotions. It would feel real. I just needed to keep acting the part long enough.

But on days when my façade wavered, I escaped to the library, knowing it was a safe place to hide. Anyone who ventured into the library would be there for a purpose, whether it be research or finding something good to read. Either way, eyes would be directed at books and not at me. I sank into a chair, resting my head in my hands. Despite my role change, I was getting tired of being on stage.

"Everything all right, Ms. Collins?" a gravelly voice asked from behind my chair.

I whipped my head up and looked over my shoulder. Mr. Nordell greeted me with a close-mouthed smile. As the high school biology teacher, I wasn't surprised to find his hands occupied with thick textbooks. His face looked worn and tired with wrinkles that aged him, but there was a kindness to his small, brown eyes that peered down at me from his rectangular glasses.

"Oh. Hi, Mr. Nordell." I had to crane my neck to look up at his lanky form, my eyes stopping briefly at his ridiculous brown-and-orange plaid bow tie. What awful colors together.

"You didn't answer my question," he said. "How are you doing, young lady?"

I let out a quiet laugh. Talk about a loaded question! My eyes glistened.

Crap. I wiped the tears away before they could

spill down on their own. I really didn't need another teacher contacting the school counselor with concern for my well-being. "I'm fine, Mr. Nordell. Really." I managed to turn the corners of my mouth upwards, hoping it passed for a smile.

"I haven't seen you around much," he commented, surprising me by maintaining the conversation. I had expected he would take his research material and return to his office. "You know, I always thought you'd end up in my AP Bio class this year."

I did, too, in fact. I always found biology fascinating, and I did well in Mr. Nordell's class when I was a sophomore. I still kind of regretted not taking the advanced course, but after Maddie died, I ended up dropping the class, not sure I would be able to handle the intensity. That was back when I was making decisions to drop a lot of things from my life.

The bell rang, giving me an excuse not to engage, but Mr. Nordell persisted.

"I have something I've been meaning to show you," he said, taking a couple of steps towards the library doors. "Stop by my classroom during lunch tomorrow. I'll tell you about it then."

Confused, I rose to my feet. "Oh… sure, ok."

Mr. Nordell nodded at me in satisfaction. "Ok, Ms. Collins, I'll see you then."

The next day, I walked past the cafeteria, finishing an apple. I walked the halls. Reaching the biology room, I knocked on the door. Mr. Nordell's calm, low voice welcomed me inside. I tossed the core in the trash and approached his desk.

"Hi," I said with uncertainty.

Mr. Nordell closed one of the thick books I'd seen him holding yesterday. "Go ahead and have a seat," he invited, pulling up a chair beside him. I didn't like the idea of sitting down. That meant this was more than just a quick chat. Tentatively, I did as he asked. I hadn't spoken much with Mr. Nordell since he was my teacher. He was just the typical boring science teacher—nice enough—but I couldn't imagine what he wanted to show me.

He conversed pleasantly with me for a few minutes about nothing in particular. Finally, I asked, "So, what did you want to show me?"

Mr. Nordell pulled a beat-up wallet from the pocket of his mustard khakis. His weathered hands flipped it open, and he pulled out a laminated photo. I could tell the photo was older because of how the corners were peeling and bubbling apart.

I accepted the photo in my hands of a woman in her late thirties, though her clothes suggested it was a couple of decades old. She was pretty enough, even with her light brown hair curled with bangs over her forehead. What touched me was the sweet smile on her face. "Is this your wife?" I asked, though I wondered why he was keeping such an outdated photo of her in his wallet. Then it dawned on me why he must be showing me this picture, even as he answered.

"Yep," Mr. Nordell said. "That's the last formal

picture I took of her, the day before we found out she had ovarian cancer. She didn't like too many picture of herself after that."

I handed the photo back to Mr. Nordell. Gingerly, he accepted it. "I'm very sorry to hear that."

"Twenty years ago," he said, leaning back in his chair with a sigh. "Death—it changes you." He made eye contact as though waiting for my response.

"Yeah, I know." My words were curt, though I spoke softly so I didn't come off disrespectful. Even though I didn't like being tricked into the topic, I wasn't about to walk out when he was speaking of his dead wife.

"I know a little something about change," he said, his gaze strong. He didn't push me to speak, though I could feel the window of opportunity cracking open. Even though the situation was a little uncomfortable, there was an aura of kindness and understanding about him.

"I'm sure you do. It must have been difficult to watch your wife pass away." I didn't know what else to say besides the generic response—although, personally, sometimes I wished people would stick to general comments instead of diving into "sage advice". Especially when they'd never experienced death.

Mr. Nordell simply nodded, his expression thoughtful. I waited a few moments, expecting him to dive into his story and tell me all about how he overcame his loss. The school counselor had probably put him up to this since she had been unable to make headway with me herself at the beginning of the school year. Or maybe Mom had called him…

Instead of talking about himself and then probing me to share the details that the whole school seemed interested in hearing, Mr. Nordell surprised me. Interlocking his fingers, he placed them on the desk. "If you ever want to hear more about that change I mentioned, stop by after school some time."

"Is… that all?" I asked, confusion touching my expression. Adults didn't normally end this topic with me so easily.

Mr. Nordell's weathered brown eyes stayed with mine. "If you'd like."

I glanced at the open classroom door, hesitating. "Ok, then," I said. "Um, bye, Mr. Nordell." Picking up my backpack, I stepped quickly into the hall, shutting the door behind me.

"*Where* were you?" Tara asked as she pulled open her front door. She stood there in sports shorts and a tank top, with her fluorescent-pink sports bra peeking out from underneath her black top. In contrast, wearing jeans and a black sweater from school today, I slid past her scowl and sat down on her couch. She followed me in earnest, plopping down next to me in a huff. "Why did you skip out on practice today? Coach was livid!"

I had no doubt Coach Robbins was indeed red

faced and furious. You pretty much had to be lying in bed puking (and doing so while on the phone with him), for Coach to forgive a missed practice. Forgive was probably too generous a word though. It was more like he would be "forced to acknowledge illness," and then you paid for it later with what could only be described as physical torment.

"I know, I know," I said, having already ignored the first phone call from him. I was not looking forward to that conversation.

"Do you know how much it sucked to be yelled at in your place? I guess he thinks I was in on it or something—which I'm totally not, since I've hardly even seen you this week during school. Where've you been?"

Knowing she wouldn't understand my new library hideout, I hesitated with my explanation. It was Monday when Mr. Nordell first spoke to me in the library and invited me to his classroom. Tuesday was when he had mentioned his wife's passing. I didn't know why, but there was something about him that made me want to listen to what he had to say. Maybe it was the way he invited without pushing, or the genuine way in which he spoke from the heart, but I wanted to hear more about his wife.

So today, Thursday, I had stepped into his classroom after school.

"Ms. Collins," he'd said, "What can I do for you?"

I swallowed once, making up my mind to press forward with the conversation. "What do you miss most about your wife?"

Mr. Nordell had immediately stopped erasing the white board and sat down with me. He talked about missing Cynthia's companionship, hearing the music she played on the piano, and smelling the food she cooked wafting through the house and welcoming him home. He talked about the laughter and conversations they shared, and the memories of raising two kids together.

I asked him if her death had changed him significantly. His response was, "You can't get hit with an emotional sledgehammer without incurring some psychological scarring." He told me to come back another day, and he would elaborate. Not once did he ask about Maddie's death or my near drowning. For once, it was just refreshing to listen to someone else share their story of love and loss. But mostly the love.

I tried to explain this to Tara, but the first thing she said from the couch was, "NERD-dell? You were hanging out with *that* old geezer?"

"Tara, really? Ok, this is why I wasn't going to tell you."

Tara's dad happened to walk into the kitchen during our conversation. He poked his head out from behind the wall. "Did you say Nordell? As in Frank Nordell?'

"Yeah, that dreary geek of a science teacher," Tara answered. "Talk about snooze-fest during tenth grade biology."

"Oh come on, he wasn't that bad. He was interesting if you were paying attention," I defended.

Mr. Davis chimed into the conversation. "Nordell is still there, huh? He was my teacher during senior year. You guys call him "NERD-dell" now? Well, that's certainly a change."

"How do you mean?" I asked.

"I'll be right back." Mr. Davis hurried down into the basement. A few minutes later, he returned with an old yearbook from twenty years ago. It was from his senior year. "See, look here," he continued, flipping through the pages. He paused at a full spread of pictures and an article highlighting Mr. Nordell. Aside from the contrast in age, I was surprised by the photos I saw, portraying a much younger Nordell with a wide smile and brightness to his eyes that made them seem larger than they actually were. Of course, that could have been due to his oversized glasses, too.

"Nordell was all the rage," Mr. Davis said, flipping a few pages to show more pictures of our teacher hanging out with students. Some of the pictures portrayed science experiments with students eagerly involved, while others were of a goofy nature with Mr. Nordell wearing a rainbow mullet wig or a ridiculous orange top hat. All of his pictures included students squeezing into the picture, eager to be a part of the memories.

"Wow, I can't believe so many kids are hanging on him, like he was cool or something," Tara interjected.

"He was," Mr. Davis said, turning to a page dedicated to teacher superlatives. He pointed to a laughing Nordell, his jaw opened wide in what appeared to be a boisterous laugh. Underneath the picture were the words: *Most likely to change the world, one laugh at a time!*

"He was well-liked by every student he encountered, and he could turn any bad day upside down. It's too bad about his wife," Mr. Davis added, closing the yearbook. "They didn't find out about her cancer until it was stage four. She passed away within a few months of her diagnosis." Tara's dad shook his head sympathetically. "The interesting thing though, is that I didn't even know Nordell *had* a wife until she became sick. Nordell was friendly and outgoing but not very open when it came to his personal life."

Considering the cherished memories and details that Mr. Nordell had shared with me already, this fact surprised me. So that was evidence of one thing that had changed about him. I continued to listen to Mr. Davis reminisce.

"I had just graduated high school when she died, so I didn't follow up with how Nordell faired after all that, though I heard back then that it hit him pretty hard. I can only imagine…" He put his arm around Tara's shoulders. "Don't know what I'd do if your mom died."

"Yeah, that would suck," Tara agreed. "Well, I'm sure that won't happen to us. That would be crazy."

I tried to ignore the bitter thoughts in my mind. I was envious of her naïve outlook on death—as if tragedy wouldn't strike her family simply because everything seemed to go right for her. I used to be like that. I used to think my life was invincible, too.

It wasn't—and I wanted now, more than ever, to visit with Mr. Nordell again.

CHAPTER TEN

The lunch bell rang. Walking down the hall on Friday, I hurried toward Mr. Nordell's room. In my haste, I didn't even see Shane until he called my name. He grabbed my arm to slow me down.

"There you are," Shane said. "Where are you going? Didn't you see my texts?"

I pulled my arm free from his grasp, not appreciating the hold. "No, I haven't had time to check my phone. I was in a hurry, actually." I noticed the irritated gleam in his eyes.

"Well, wherever you were going, you need to cancel. Austin just had free period and is driving back with pizza. He's meeting us in the senior quad. Come on." He took my arm again, pulling me in the other direction.

"Hey, stop it," I said, freeing my limb once again. He wasn't gripping me hard, but I didn't appreciate him intervening in my plans—plans that were more important to me than eating cheap pizza. The annoyance in Shane's expression returned.

"What's the matter with you?" he asked. His dark eyebrows push downwards with disappointment. "We've hardly hung out all week. You keep disappearing." His expression turned. His fingers caressed the side of my face and, with a softer voice, he said, "You ok?"

At his touch, my own annoyance faltered, as did my words. I could admit that I wasn't being much of a girlfriend to him this past week... or whatever our relationship was at the moment. Wasn't I supposed to look forward to hanging out with him, rather than feel obligated?

I paid attention around me for a moment, catching the infatuated ogling happening from a number of girls passing by. *You are so lucky,* their expressions seemed to say when they caught my eyes. What was wrong with me that I couldn't appreciate being with Shane? Superficial or not, it was easier to be a part of this dating limelight than spotlighted by grief. I didn't want to lose that.

I gently removed his fingers from my face but made a point of holding his hand. "Yeah, I'm fine." Burying a sigh, I turned my back on Mr. Nordell's classroom. My conversation with him would have to wait until after the weekend now. "All right, let's go get some pizza."

That night, we crept along the fence of an apartment building, hoping to gain access to the community hot tub. Tara and Austin led the way, followed by Ben and Landon, and a girl named Kate. She was better friends with Ben than with any of us. Shane and I brought up the rear. As suspected, since it was just past ten PM, the gate was locked and the pool area empty.

A part of me hoped we would just call it a night. We had already stayed after school for the boys' basketball game. After showers, we met up at Shane's house for dinner and a movie in his home-theater room. With the basement designed in stadium seating and a projector, it'd been nice to sink into his thick leather couches and relax. Now, however, I was anxious about getting caught breaking into the apartment complex—but I also didn't want to be the first to bail. Everyone had given me a hard time at lunch today while we ate pizza in the quad, talking about how I had pretty much ditched them all week.

"Looks like we'll have to jump the fence after all," Austin said, assessing the height.

"It's only seven-feet high or so." Ben tested the strength of the iron fence by jumping and applying some of his weight. It seemed sturdy enough. One by one, we took turns hopping over the fence, us girls utilizing someone's knee for extra height and stability. The sharp, pointed ends at the top of the fence were a little trickier to hurdle, but with help, we all managed to jump over unscathed.

We had to rely on the nearby street lamps to provide dim lighting around the hot tub, but it was enough. We stripped our sweats and T-shirts down to our swimsuits and slipped into the hot tub. Fortunately, the water was still warm. Kate hit the switch for the jets, blasting us with a spray of bubbles.

"Man, this was the best idea ever," Shane said, sinking up to his chin.

"Yeah, no kidding," Austin agreed. "Not a bad way to celebrate our win today." There was a chorus of approval from our group. My nerves aside, I had to admit that the hot tub soothed my aching muscles like magic.

"Well," Landon said, leaning over the edge of the hot tub to grab his duffle bag. "Time for the essentials." He unzipped it and pulled out a six-pack. He popped the cans off the plastic rings and handed them out.

I shook my head and turned down Landon's offer, hearing Shane's can crack open with a *hiss* beside me. I watched Tara accept the beer, though her eyes flicked towards me for just an instant before she pulled back on the metal tab. Shane took a gulp and slipped his arm around my shoulders. "What? You're not gonna drink tonight?"

"Not any night," I corrected, ignoring the smirks from Kate and Landon. Shane chuckled before taking another sip.

"All right, all right," he said in a patronizing tone. His wide smile showed he was humored by my statement. I wasn't sure what he thought was so funny. "Just checking if you had changed your mind yet."

"Come *on*. Lighten up, Allie." Austin complained, nuzzling Tara's neck. She laughed, pulling away like it tickled, though her eyes caught mine with a touch of apprehension.

"Hey, ease up, man," Shane said to his friend,

sitting up against the hot tub. "She doesn't want a drink right now. Big deal."

I directed my words at Austin. "If you cared about your position on the basketball team as much as you appear, I'd be more cautious if I were you. If any of you get caught," my eyes darted to Tara, "you're going to be kicked off the team, or at least suspended from a game or two. Are you really willing to jeopardize that?" As wrestlers, this could affect Ben and Landon, too.

Tara blindsided me with her comment. She almost said the words under her breath, but not quite. "What's it to you? It's not like you care about our team anyway."

My mouth opened, reflecting on the grueling training I'd endured five days a week for over a month. "It was *one* practice, Tara. I missed *one* practice." I couldn't believe Tara was ganging up on me with Austin. She had a tendency to be outspoken, but there was something more scornful about her words tonight, and they were aimed at me.

"You're totally off your game," Tara said, placing her beer on the side of the hot tub.

"What are you talking about? I kill myself during practice!" I could feel a rush of heat touch my face, fueled by disbelief and hurt. I may not be doing a lot of things right this year, but I knew how to push myself.

Tara shook her head. "Sure, you're *training*, but when it comes to the team—to the game—you're still stuck in your own little world. Take Wednesday's game, for instance. You were out there on the court, but it's like you were just going through the motions. Yes, we won, but where's that fire and drive you used to have? I mean, seriously, did that part of you drown with your cousin?"

Tara's hand slapped over her mouth, her eyes wide. She obviously hadn't meant to say those words, but with how fast they slipped from her lips, she'd had them locked and loaded. "I—I mean…" Her words stuttered, her voice soft and uncertain.

I clenched my jaw, refusing to let the sting of her words show on my face. Still, I had to swallow the lump in my throat, praying the burning in my eyes wouldn't result in tears. I watched Tara's face crumple, an apology forming in her gaze.

The expressions on everyone's face showed their discomfort, their eyes looking back and forth between Tara and me. I couldn't believe she'd said that to me, even if there was some truth to her words. She was right, of course. Even *I* could tell that my love for the game—the passion that had fueled my adrenaline for years—was lacking this season. I was trying, I really was. But a person could only fake that devotion and intensity for so long. Still, Tara didn't need to point it out to everyone, not like this.

I stood up and stepped out of the hot tub, wrapping my towel around my torso as I stalked off towards the fence with my clothes in hand.

"Allie—Allie, wait!" Tara called out. From the sounds of water splashing behind me, I knew she, and perhaps Shane, were scrambling out of the hot tub, too. I didn't know where I was going—it wasn't like I had keys to either of the two cars we had carpooled in.

"Hold on, Allie!" Shane's voice also called. I reached the fence and dropped my towel long enough to slip my clothes back on. By the time I finished dressing, Tara and Shane had caught up to me.

"I didn't mean it," Tara said. "Really, I—" Her words were cut off when we heard a short siren on the other side of the fence behind us. Red and blue lights flashed in our eyes.

"Cops!" Austin shouted. All of them leaped out of the tub, ditching their beer cans but snatching their clothes. They sprinted to the far side of the fence. Tara, Shane, and I followed suit, ignoring the cop who stepped out of his vehicle.

"Hey, you kids there!" he hollered. "Hold it!"

Oh, crap!

My heart thumped in my chest as I took off after the others. The cop yelled at us again. I chanced a look over my shoulder, seeing him running along the fence towards us.

Kate, Ben, and Landon had already scaled the fence and were far down the road. Austin was on the other side of the fence, waiting for Tara. Shane lifted her enough so she could pull herself up and over, letting Austin catch her. Then Shane gave me a boost. I swung my leg over the top, intending for my jump to carry me through. But my sweatpants caught on the sharp, pointed edge, grazing my thigh. The unexpected jolt threw off my landing, and I twisted my right ankle. I grimaced in pain just before Shane landed next to me. He pulled me to my feet while I hobbled after him for a few steps.

"Stop!" The cop was fifty feet away, pointing his flashlight at us as he drew near. Shane swore under his breath, holding my bicep as he tugged me alongside him. Adrenaline kicked in, providing a low anesthetic for the pain. I ignored my body's attempts to slow me down, warning me of my injured ankle.

I shook Shane off. "I'm fine! I can run!"

We had no idea which direction everyone else had escaped. We cut across the road, aiming to lodge ourselves between the close-knit houses along the street—and to escape the cop's view. Glancing over my shoulder, my face fell in dismay. He had seen where we'd turned and was gaining on us! Whatever happened to the overweight, donut-eating cops everyone stereotyped? We could have really used one of them at the moment, instead of this guy, who was fit and chasing us like he had something to prove.

Just let us go already! I wanted to shout. I hoped he'd consider us good and scared and surrender the pursuit, but fortune was not on our side. Not only that, but we could also hear him on his radio, calling for backup.

Really? You need backup?

"Come on, come on!" Shane's hushed voice called to me as we leaped over bushes and slipped passed trees. A wave of familiarity hit me, realizing it had only been a few weeks since we'd been chased on the golf course for our paintballing stunt. I wondered if we'd be so lucky this time.

We stumbled back onto another street, running at a diagonal to hide between another row of houses. As we crossed the curb, my damaged ankle finally gave out and I fell to my knees with a grunt. Shane had already made it between the houses before he looked back and saw me struggling. Just up the road, a cop car flashed its lights, heading my way—and not fifteen feet behind me was Hero-cop.

"Shane, run! Get out of here!" I cried. He hesitated until I shouted again. "Go!" On my feet once more, I turned right. My crippled run slowed me down, but at least I was drawing the cop on foot in my direction, away from Shane. I knew that if someone were to get caught tonight, it was better that it be me.

Not thirty seconds later, Hero-cop wrapped his large hand around my bicep, whipping me to a halt. Without even giving me a chance to face him, he ordered me to my knees.

"Put your hands behind your back," he commanded, his voice booming with authority. His handcuffs clanked together with anticipation. I kneeled on the curb, my eyes catching the curious onlookers driving by and a woman peeking through her blinds. I tried to ignore their stares, my face flushed and my breaths heaving in my chest. Some teenagers driving by hollered at me with laughter, mocking my arrest. I kept my eyes down, anger and adrenaline keeping me heated, despite the cold weather wrapping its icy breath around me.

With the handcuffs locked in place, the cop pulled me to my feet, turning me around to face him and his unwarranted "backup". This cop was definitely younger—probably new in his career, which explained his zealous chase.

"What have we got here, Jared?" the second cop said, assessing my appearance. He looked more seasoned and didn't strut the way Hero-cop did. "They gave you a pretty decent chase, huh?"

Hero-cop shook his head with a laugh. His chest puffed out as he spoke, highlighting his muscled frame. "Nah, it was nothin'."

I rolled my eyes at his ego. I couldn't help myself from speaking. "Yeah, good for you for catching an injured seventeen-year-old *girl*." I didn't break away from his glare. "Fantastic job." His frown hardened, while the other cop suppressed a smile behind one hand. I knew I shouldn't have said it. It certainly wouldn't help my situation, but the anger I'd felt at my so-called friends needed to be redirected somewhere.

"Have a seat," Hero-cop said, gripping my arm and yanking me backwards. I landed on my rear, seated on the edge of the curb.

Whatever. I probably deserved that.

The other cop winked at me with a grin. Confused but happy for a possible ally, I let a smile slip in return, while Hero-cop flipped through a notepad.

"Caught this one and a few of her friends drinking inside Jordan Apartments. The ol' hot tub break in again," Hero-cop said, glancing at me like I was being scolded.

"For what it's worth, I wasn't drinking." I tossed my head to knock strands of hair away from my eyes.

"We'll see about that," Hero-cop said. "Evan, I need to grab the Breathalyzer from your car. Be right back."

Officer Evan nodded. Turning to me, he asked, "So what's your name?"

"Allie Collins."

"You have ID on you, Allie?"

"No, I don't." I'd left my purse, with my wallet and phone, inside Shane's car. I wondered how those guys were doing, assuming they had made their way back to the cars by now.

"Well," Officer Evan started.

Hero-cop cut him off. "Guess that means you'll be under arrest so your parents can come and claim you from jail—if they want."

I suppressed the urge to retort with another rude remark. I knew at this point I shouldn't press my luck, even if this cop thought he was hardcore or something. It was obviously a slow night for actual criminals if he was willing to take the pursuit this far.

"Breathe into this," he instructed. I blew into the tube with zero hesitancy, knowing I'd pass the test. Hero-cop seemed disappointed with the results. Bringing me to my feet, Officer Evan escorted me into the back of his police car. I'd never sat in one before. The doors slammed shut. I felt claustrophobic, staring at the caged wall that barred me from the front seats.

How did I get myself into this mess? I wondered, watching the two cops getting into a discussion outside my window. Reflecting on the recent scares over the past few weeks, I couldn't help but realize that Shane and my new friends were the common factor in these repeat scenarios.

Both cops situated themselves in the front seat. Hero-cop's frown deepened, but he didn't say anything more to me—not even when Officer Evan dropped him off at his car. I did a quick scan of the streets but didn't see Shane or Austin's cars.

Once we were alone, the officer turned his head towards me and said, "I convinced Officer Harmon to let me take you home. You obviously weren't drinking. Consider this a warning."

I nodded my head. "Thanks. I appreciate that." I gave him my home address. After a minute of driving, Officer Evan broke the silence.

"So let me guess. You're a senior?"

"Yeah."

"You thinking about college?"

"Of course," I answered. "I'm still just doing applications and all that." I could feel his next question. "Fresno State, maybe."

"Northern California. Nice choice. So what high school do you attend?"

I closed my mouth, eying the back of the police officer's head. If he wasn't arresting me, he didn't need my personal details. I folded my arms. "Is this the whole 'good cop-bad cop' scenario where you convince me to give up my friends? Because I'm not going to do that."

A moment of silence—then he let out a laugh. "Relax. It's called making small talk." He looked over his shoulder at me through the grate, his expression humored. "I'm beginning to think kids these days don't know how to do that anymore if it doesn't involve texting." He returned his eyes to the road.

I let out a sound of contempt. "I can handle small talk. I just don't like being tricked."

"No tricks here," Officer Evans said. "But I can understand you being cautious. It's the 'stranger-danger' concept we try and ingrain in little kids. Besides, we all have things we'd rather keep to ourselves. Right?"

I stopped talking after that.

CHAPTER ELEVEN

"What were you doing breaking into an apartment complex anyway?" Mom asked, her arms folded across her chest and her posture rigid. She closed the front door behind me.

"There wasn't actually any breaking…" I started to say, trying to ease my way towards my bedroom around the corner.

"And why would you think it's ok to stick around while your friends drank?" Mom's voice rose higher with each question. At this rate, I expected she might reach the level of "only dogs can hear you". I almost made a joke about that, but held my tongue. She was evidently not in the mood.

"About them being my friends… I'll admit that's a little in question these days…" I took another side step, adding a bit of distance between us. My friendship with Tara and the rest of them would take a little time to figure out, though at the moment, I was still riding on adrenaline from being chased. And my ankle throbbed.

Mom threw up her hands. "Well, that's obvious! I can't believe they all ditched you and left you to take the rap." She let out a disgruntled sigh and then mumbled with a shake of her head, "And to think I thought that boy was so nice…."

Thinking about Shane and remembering the concern in his eyes as he saw me fall, I felt like I needed to put a plug in for him. I was the one who had told him to leave, after all. "They didn't ditch me on purpose. We all split up after we jumped the—" Mom's glare made me pause, and I mumbled the last word, "—fence."

"Allie, it is very late—and I know your sisters are wide awake, listening through their door." We heard a quick thunk from the hallway, indicating Mom's statement was correct. I tried not to laugh, but the sound escaped anyway. My sisters were so nosy.

Mom sighed. "When I told you I hoped you would hang out with your friends again, I didn't mean like this. What were you thinking?" Mom put a hand to her forehead. "Never mind. We'll discuss this later. Just please go to bed, and don't expect to have any plans this weekend."

I had figured as much.

With no phone and being grounded from leaving the house, the rest of the weekend continued without incident, other than Shane stopping by to return my phone Saturday morning. I was on the couch, elevating my foot to ease the blue swelling, when Mom opened the front door. I couldn't hear the conversation, but whatever murmured exchange took place was short and to the point. Mom passed by the living room with my phone in her hands. I eyed the phone before checking her expression.

She didn't even slow her stride. "Don't even think about it."

With my phone locked away, I had plenty of time to wonder how the night had played out for Shane and the others. I also had time to think about my friendship with Tara. Her words regarding my lack of heart in basketball still hurt. Our relationship seemed to be deteriorating quickly, and I felt a sense of loss. Whether it was her dating Austin or my failed efforts to normalize myself since the accident, things were changing between us and I didn't like it, or even know what to do about it.

An hour later, Leah and Taylor left the house to catch a matinee. One minute after the door shut, it opened again and Taylor reappeared.

"Did you forget something?" I asked.

Taylor glanced around before hurrying to my side. Her grin turned devious as she slipped a folded piece of paper into my hands. "Better not let Mom see." With those instructions, she flew out the door just as Mom rounded the corner. I made a fist, wadding the paper inside my hand.

"Was that Taylor? I thought Mrs. Stevens picked them up already. They're going to be late to the movie." Mom opened the door, peering outside, and then waved as the car pulled out of the driveway.

"She… forgot her wallet," I said, restraining my curiosity as the corners of the folded paper dug into my palm.

Mom shut the door and finished buttoning her blue dress shirt. I noticed she had also changed into black slacks and had applied makeup.

"Are you going to the office today?" I asked, though I already knew the answer.

Mom grabbed a stack of papers from the table and shoved them into her work bag. "Yes, I need to go in for a few hours, unfortunately."

"But you worked the last two weekends, too."

She ran a hand through her hair, taking a moment to pull through a tangled end. "I know, I'm sorry. It's been crazy at the firm this month—absolutely nuts. There's a big case going to trial, and truly, the attorneys are hopeless without us…" She sighed, pausing to slip on her shoes.

I didn't know much about law, but I knew any firm would be lucky to have my mom as their paralegal. She didn't put up with nonsense, as I was experiencing firsthand myself.

"Anyway, it's just for the afternoon. I'll be back for dinner. Thai food tonight?"

"Sure."

"Ok, then. Stay off your ankle, all right? And by that, I mean, you better not leave the house." She tipped her head and gave me a strong, pointed look.

"I'm not going anywhere."

"And he better not come in," Mom added.

"Ok already!"

As soon as Mom left, I stretched open my fingers.

Unfolding the wad of paper, I saw a handwritten note and, after skimming the bottom, saw it was from Shane:

Hey, Beautiful,
Sorry about last night. Can't believe that dumb cop cuffed you! If it makes you feel any better, you looked hot getting arrested. Hope your ankle is ok. I'm tempted to stop by your window tonight to see you, but I know you will tell me that's a bad idea. I'll give your Mom some space before I try stopping by again. (She hates me, doesn't she?) Catch you at school.
~Shane
PS: I'm sitting and waiting in the bushes. I texted your sister, and she said she was leaving the house soon. It's freezing out here. Oh well. I'm sure you'll make it up to me later.

I folded the note and tucked it into my back pocket. While I knew our relationship lacked in a lot of ways, the note still made me smile… and also roll my eyes, considering the last line. I wondered if he was still out there—and if he was, hopefully Shane had parked away from the house. If not, he was probably getting an earful from Mom right now.

I thought about slipping outside to check for him—but I didn't want to break Mom's trust, especially if her leaving for work was actually a test. Maybe she was hiding around the corner, waiting to see what I would do next.

Not likely. She really did take her job seriously and had enough to worry about without me causing drama. I kept the door locked until my sisters came home.

By early Monday morning, my phone seemed heavier in my hands when I saw the bombardment of new text messages from Tara. They were a stream of apologies that had been sent throughout the weekend, in between missed calls. I softened a little, reminding myself that I'd said my fair share of rude things to people in the heat of the moment. Barely making it to school on time, I hobbled out of my car and hurried to class without a chance to talk to her or Shane.

The rumors were back. I could feel it. With all the experience I'd gained since the beginning of the school year, my peripheral vision had a knack for picking up on the questionable looks from students. As I limped into my first period class, a spray of whispering showered the room—only pausing when my eyes caught the murmuring culprits looking back at me. I could barely focus on what my English teacher was saying. Instead, an anxious weight in my chest made me feel self-conscious and uncertain. People were talking about me again, and I was sure it had something to do with the weekend incident.

I found Taylor after my English class, assuming she would know if anything was going on. She liked keeping up with the latest happenings at school.

"So did you hear what happened to you this

weekend?" she asked, her eyes wide in exaggeration. She grinned when I folded my arms.

"Just get it over with. What's everyone saying about me this time?" I asked.

"Well, it's more exciting than what *really* happened." Taylor shut her locker.

"It always is. Just tell me."

"Ok, but you're going to be mad." At my impatient gesture, she continued. "The rumor going around is that you cheated on Shane with some random guy in a hot tub—"

"Of course," I said, placing one hand on my hip "And?"

"And then the cops arrested you for drinking, and you spent the night in jail."

I threw my head back in frustration. "For real? Why does anyone believe this crap?" I was really getting sick of high school.

Taylor walked with me. "It doesn't matter if it's believable—if it's fun to *assume* it's true, then that's more entertaining than the truth itself." I frowned at her words, knowing she had a point. The trend of drama-filled reality shows, with ratings skyrocketing when an episode was fueled with deceit and betrayal, proved that much.

"I have to say, graduating high school and leaving all this behind is looking more appealing every day."

"That's mean," Taylor said. "What about Leah and me?"

"Well, of course, I'll miss you guys. Even if you *are*

overly boy crazy."

Taylor shrugged, not the least bit concerned about my opinion. "You're the one with the boyfriend," she countered. I couldn't really argue there, although the term "boyfriend" seemed too formal for Shane and me and, according to the newest rumor, I no longer had one anyway. "At least you still have basketball."

I hesitated with my response and then settled for, "Yeah—I guess."Taylor's eyebrows curved in confusion, or maybe disappointment… Then something, or someone, of interest caught her attention. Just as I turned my head, a pair of soft lips fixed on mine, pressing against me with determination. I staggered backwards in surprise, pulling away from the sneak attack.

Shane grinned back at me. Taylor put a hand to her mouth and giggled. "I'll let you handle that on your own. Later, Allie!"

"What was that for?" I asked, looking around in embarrassment to see if anyone had noticed. I really didn't need the extra attention. As expected, kids slowed their pace, rubbernecking when they walked by, as if trying to catch a glimpse of a car accident. With news going around that I cheated on Shane, they were probably hoping for a dramatic end to our relationship—especially the usual crowd gawking at him with lovesick eyes.

Shane laughed. "Just trying to eradicate the rumors, or at least the one about us breaking up." His face twisted into a mock-scowl as he pointed his finger at me. Speaking louder, he said sternly, "And don't cheat on me again!"

I grabbed his finger with one hand, using my other to push his chest backwards until he knocked into a locker. "Stop it!" I hissed. "That is the *opposite* of helping!"

Shane chuckled, grabbing both my hands with his. He looked down, his perfect smile diffusing me—until he spoke again. "Oh, people need to lighten up. Let's be honest—why would you ever cheat on me?"

My mouth gaped open as I folded my arms across my chest. "You are unbelievable."

"Thank you."

"That wasn't a compliment." I broke free from his grasp. "You really are more attractive when you're not talking." Despite his arrogant laughter, I added, "Speaking of which, thanks for the note on Saturday."

"I thought you might like that. How's the ankle?"

"Sore, but I'm mobile enough."

"So when should I try and win your mom over?" Shane wrapped his arms around me and pulled my body into his. My cheeks flushed, still feeling the questioning gazes.

"Um," I said, peeling myself away from his grasp, "you might want to give that some time. She doesn't have the most forgiving nature…" I'd witnessed it firsthand after Dad cheated and he tried to reconcile. Not that I blamed her, and of course, that issue was on a much larger scale than this. But still, I knew she wouldn't make it easy on Shane to change her opinion of him. "Hey, I gotta get to class. I'll catch up with you at lunch." I steered away from Shane and all the whispers trailing behind me.

Tara and I finally ran into each other. We sat in the senior quad with our usual group, including Austin, Kate, Ben, and Landon. This was the first time all of us were together again since Friday night's fiasco. Tara greeted me with a tight squeeze before jumping into her apologies again.

"It's ok," I interrupted. "Let's just start over, all right? So what happened to you guys after we split?" I asked.

"Austin and I stuck together," Tara said, while Austin's arms wrapped securely around her waist. That fact didn't surprise me.

"We turned the corner and ran half a block before we circled back to the cars," Austin chimed in. "We wanted to wait for you and Shane, but were afraid the cop would return and start asking questions."

Kate spoke. "Austin and Tara picked us up when they saw us sneaking around Shane's car." She gestured at Ben and Landon. "We were waiting for you guys to get back."

"We kept driving by until we saw Shane return," Tara said. "We were so scared when we realized you weren't with him! We heard Shane's version through text messages, but I want to hear it from you. Give us the details!"

I gave them a brief rundown of the evening, including twisting my ankle, the overzealous cop chasing me down, and the mellow cop intervening and giving me a break.

"It's a good thing *you* were caught and not us," Landon said with relief in his voice. While I'd had the same thought—understanding that their consequences would have been more severe than mine with alcohol on their breaths—I didn't appreciate the statement coming from him. He was the dummy who had brought the beer in the first place.

"Is that your way of saying 'thank you?'" I asked, not hiding the annoyance in my tone.

Landon seemed taken aback by my response. "Why would I thank you? I got away just fine. You're the one that apparently couldn't jump the fence." He indicated my bruised ankle.

"If you hadn't brought beer, that cop wouldn't have bothered chasing us in the first place!" Fuming, I glared at him. "I could have turned you in—any of you—" I added, my gaze circling, "—but I didn't."

"Not turning us in should be a *given*, not a favor," Austin said. "That's what *friends* do. Look, if you want a 'thank you'—"

"Austin, quit being an idiot," Shane interrupted.

Both Austin and I ignored him. "No, that's not the point. I just..." I let out a huff of frustration, unsure what I wanted. I was irritated at them for dragging me into the situation after I had even warned them, and mad at myself for not stepping out when I was uncomfortable with it. As for them being my *friends*... I looked around the disgruntled group. The term *friend was* being used as loosely as *boyfriend.* "Forget it." I abandoned my sandwich, ignoring Tara calling after me. When Shane caught up to me, I resisted his touch and asked for some time alone.

Shuffling into the gym, I hugged the sidelines while my teammates started the usual warm up by jogging around the court. Seating myself on the bottom bleacher, I put my feet out in front of me to elevate my ankle. Walking around on it all day had increased the swelling again, almost immobilizing the joint. I should have borrowed crutches, but I didn't want to draw more attention.

"Collins!" Coach Robbins voice boomed as he pushed his way through the double doors. I noticed my teammates slowing their jog as they made another lap around the court, all eyes watching Coach's face with anticipation.

I grimaced. I was about to get reamed.

"What kind of stupid stunt did you pull on Friday?" He looked down at me from his towering height, eying my blue-and-purple ankle in annoyance and with zero sympathy.

I dropped my gaze uneasily. I was used to him hollering at me on the court. That didn't bother me because it was part of the game, but in this situation, when it came to my personal life, his tone put me on edge.

Unsure of how much gossip had circulated back to him, I settled for, "I jumped a fence and fell."

"After being chased by cops?" he interjected.

Yikes. So he had heard a few details. "There was a misunderstanding," I began.

"A misunderstanding? Well, we're about to clear that up right now. Principal Hayden wants to see you in the athletic department. Let's go." He pointed to the assistant coach. "Jenkins, have them hit the drills."

The athletics department and the principal? Now this was really getting out of hand. It was one thing for students to spread talk amongst themselves, but bringing in the school authorities was another. My stomach turned as I rose to my feet. My eyes flickered to Tara's, who was watching the scene while chewing on her bottom lip. My sisters' concerned expressions also touched mine before I looked away. I focused on walking out of the gym, a feeling of dread weighing me down.

Coach Robbins remained a step ahead of me the whole time, not pausing to hold the swinging door open for me as I limped behind. Not that I expected it. He didn't believe in displaying a softer approach to girls than boys. According to him, training boys and girls should not hold different standards.

As we entered the office, Principal Hayden sat in a chair next to Mr. Knox, the athletic director. The principal gestured to the two empty chairs across from them.

"Hi, Allie. Have a seat please," Principal Hayden

said. His expression was kind, yet hinting that our conversation was of a more serious nature. "Coach Robbins, join us, of course."

I took my seat among the three adults, feeling like a young child in big trouble.

Folding his hands into one another and placing them on the desk between us, Principal Hayden began. "So, Allie, it seems we need to have a discussion."

That much was obvious.

He continued. "There's a rumor going around that you were involved in some drinking and an arrest this weekend. Is there any truth to that?"

"No," I stated, my face flushing with heat from the inquiry. "I wasn't arrested. An officer just… took me home." I had a hard time maintaining eye contact. No matter what I said, there would be more questions. I could see it in their scrutinizing gazes.

"Why did the officer feel the need to take you home?" Mr. Knox asked, one eyebrow raised.

"I was—"

"Were you drunk?" Coach Robbins accused.

"Of course not. I wasn't even the one drinking." My fists clenched, realizing I'd slipped up with my word choice.

"So others students with you were drinking. Who were they?"

At my hesitated response, Principal Hayden jumped in, his voice calm and serious. "Allie, this is very important that you tell the truth here. If there were students who were involved with underage drinking—especially if they are part of the athletics' program—we need to know so this can be handled appropriately. Students need to understand that this sort of behavior is not tolerated." He rubbed his chin before adding, "Even from star athletes." His word choice led me to believe he had a hunch of who was with me that night.

I wanted to rephrase my answer and tell them that no one was drinking—that we'd only been chased by the cops for using a hot tub after hours, but I knew they wouldn't believe me now. If I told them about the other students involved, every one of them might be suspended. They (and the rest of the student population), would hate me and call me a snitch. Still… they only had my word to rely on. Even if they questioned Mom, who knew Shane was involved, they couldn't prove anything without me.

"So what can you tell us, Allie?" Mr. Knox prompted, his tone softer and coaxing. "Can you help us out here?"

"I—um…" I stuttered in thought, still undecided. After the last two confrontations with that group of "friends," I knew I didn't owe them anything. In fact, this would be an easy way to get back at them. Although, I'd have to decide if I wanted to exclude Shane and Tara from the name-dropping. But no… Aside from not wanting to face the wrath of the other students for ratting someone out, loyalty was something I valued in relationships. When Dad betrayed Mom and left us, I knew I would never be like him—would never turn my back on the relationships in my life. Even though my relationships with Tara and Shane were struggling, I couldn't bring myself to tell on them.

With three pairs of eyes watching me, all belonging to school authorities, I slowly shook my head. "I'm sorry, but I can't help you."

Principal Hayden's nose flared, while Mr. Knox let out a breath of frustrated air. Coach Robbins kept his arms folded across his chest, staring at me with disapproval. Though, if he made the assumption that Tara was likely involved, I sensed a bit of relief in his eyes for my silence. He wouldn't want one of his captains suspended from this Friday's game against our top rival.

The disappointed silence felt unbearable. I wasn't a kid that got in trouble. I'd never been sent to the principal's office. Quite the opposite—most teachers seemed to like me and consider me a "breath of fresh air" from the usual troublemakers in class.

Mr. Knox spoke first. "Well, Allie, if you are choosing to withhold information from this incident, then I have no choice but to recommend suspension from this week's game."

It was the rival game. I'd be letting down the whole team if I didn't play. "I don't understand," I said. At the same time, Coach Robbins leaned forward in his chair, his voice a touch louder as he directed words at our athletics' director.

"Now see here, Will. I don't see how that's necessary." His face reddened, and I knew it was a struggle for him to keep his tone level.

"That's not fair. I wasn't drinking," I restated. "What you heard about me today came from a rumor someone spread."

"A rumor that proved true in some regard," Principal Hayden commented. He turned to my coach. "I have to agree with Will. We need to set an example that this kind of behavior will not be tolerated." He cut off my protest, adding, "Whether it be drinking or covering up these inappropriate activities."

There was no getting out of it. I would be benched from the game and hurting my teammates for something I didn't do. Now, other students would assume the rumor was true, and that I was being punished for my misdeeds.

There was no cure to this virus.

CHAPTER TWELVE

Whether I caught people talking about me or not, I could feel the words hanging in the air. The news that I'd been benched spread like a wick to dynamite, slithering along until it exploded, chucking rumored debris all throughout the school. As with all rumors, the general idea rooted itself like the trunk of a tree, allowing branches of gossip and untruths to grow in every direction.

"She cheated on Shane…"

"She was arrested for a DUI…"

"The coach is revoking her as Captain…"

Seeking sanctuary, I skipped lunch the next day, heading for Mr. Nordell's classroom.

"Hello there, Ms. Collins," he said after I knocked on the door. "I wondered when you'd be back."

I slipped off my backpack and seated myself in the available chair next to him, as if it were placed ready and waiting for my arrival. "I was going to come sooner but…"

"But you got yourself in some trouble over the weekend."

I flushed, ready to defend myself.

Mr. Nordell winked at me. "Oh, don't you worry now. I don't believe one thing about that."

I sighed, wrinkling my forehead in frustration. "The rumors never stop. Just when I think I can fly under the radar, someone throws another one out there."

"Some people like to keep negative attention off them by pointing it at others," Mr. Nordell offered.

"It just seems like, ever since Maddie died…" I stopped. I hadn't intended to talk about her. The recent talk going around school had nothing to do with her. Yet, her name escaped my lips all the same.

He smiled. "Don't let people distract you from growing the way you need to."

"I don't know that I'm growing from Maddie's death. I feel just the opposite, like I've lost a part of who I used to be. I feel stuck."

"Well, that's part of your problem right there, if you don't mind me saying so." He paused, waiting for my approval to continue.

"Go ahead," I said, my curiosity peaked.

"You're trying to be the Allie you were before you almost drowned—before your cousin died. Think about a soldier who was maimed in war, or a person who lost a limb because of an accident. They don't get to have that body part back. They don't *get* to be the person they once were—not physically, and certainly not emotionally. It's not possible."

I pondered his words for a moment while he continued.

"Like soldiers and accident victims, lives can be altered in a matter of moments. Those that become instant amputees have to prepare for prosthetic limbs, rehab, therapy… It would be foolish to believe that our experiences in life don't shape us in one way or another." Mr. Nordell paused again, studying me. "You're not originally from Portland, are you?"

"No, I moved from Danville, California three years ago."

"California… so you are familiar with Yosemite then?"

I laughed out loud, a rush of memories touching my mind. "It was pretty much my backyard. Yosemite is gorgeous." Reflecting on the frequent camping trips we used to take as a family, I added, "There's nothing like it."

Mr. Nordell flipped open his laptop. He pulled up pictures of Yosemite Valley, pointing to the carved, granite cliffs, including the infamous Half Dome and El Capitan. "Did you know that before Yosemite became this magnificent valley, that it was just a meadow?"

I nodded my head. "I had to do a report on the formation of Yosemite in fourth grade. I learned all about how it formed from molten rock and glaciers."

The science teacher in Mr. Nordell seemed to perk up. "Now imagine, if it were possible, that Yosemite had resisted this change—that it hadn't allowed nature to take its course in molding and shaping that meadow." He scrolled through more breathtaking photos, pausing on each one. "We would not have this picturesque, remarkable valley that we cherish today. Now let me ask you one more question—how long did this formation take?"

"Millions of years," I answered. "It was a very slow process."

"Yes, very slow indeed…" He enlarged a picture of Half Dome, the granite crest an inspiring sight. Mr. Nordell's voice softened. "We may admire the end product, but do we respect the processes that lead to its creation?" He closed the laptop. "Allie," he began.

The use of my first name caught my attention.

"It's ok to deal with life-changing events at your own pace."

I furrowed my eyebrows, restraining the tears. "But it feels like I'm holding people back, like I'm constantly making people uncomfortable or unhappy because—you're right." My eyes met his with a flash of understanding. "I'm not who I used to be." More to myself than anyone, I whispered the words again because it felt good, in a way, to say it out loud. "I'm not who I used to be…"

Mr. Nordell patted my hand. "Perhaps there is more truth in that statement than you have realized." I gave a slight nod when he paused. "You need to get better for you, not for others. If people in your life are not willing to wait for you to heal, perhaps you need to consider the importance of that relationship. Time will tell."

Benched. I couldn't even remember the last time I sat out in a game for more than a quick breather, let alone for an entire game. It was an odd feeling, at the end of that week, watching our rival game played from a seated position.

Leading up to the game, the team had been on edge. I could feel it every practice as they prepped for Friday's home game. Even if the principal and athletics director hadn't forced Coach Robbins to bench me, my twisted ankle would have prevented me from playing anyway. Regardless of the reason, my absence amplified Coach's foul mood. I came to each practice to support my team, but I could feel (and hear) Coach's frustration at having to readjust the lineup and focus on set plays, rather than allow the familiar improvisation between my sisters, the other starters, and me.

During the first half of the game, as I watched my teammates from my seated position, I waited for the moment of envy to arrive. I expected to feel antsy and eager to get back on the court. However, as I watched the points bounce back and forth, evenly climbing the scoreboard, those feelings didn't come. I observed the game with the interest of a spectator, cheering extra loud for my sisters and feeling proud of the way they could soundlessly read each other's moves, and I joined the chorus of "boos" from the audience when a member of the rival team executed a cheap shot at one of our players.

Still, from my spot on the bench, I soon found myself watching the game as if through glass. At times, the game seemed muted in my head. I watched Coach's aggravated yells when one of my teammates screwed up a play (comical really, like an adult having a tantrum with the way his face flushed red, and how he stomped his large, heavy foot), and I noted the dejected expression on the player's face when she was benched as penance. The "swoosh" of the basketball through the net seemed hushed and lacking the charged excitement that normally accompanied each score. Granted, I wasn't the one making the shot. Still, something inside me felt different tonight. The feeling followed me through the conclusion of the game.

"That was the sweetest win ever!" Tara cheered, sweeping her mess of curls out of her face and tightening her ponytail.

"Congrats," I said, offering a high-five. Her hand made contact with mine. Then she leaned in, gripping my shoulder and whispered, "You're a freakin' rockstar for not giving up our names to Principal Hayden. Love you for that! I totally owe you one. We all do."

I simply nodded, stepping away when Austin found her and scooped her into his arms. The rest of the gym bustled with teammates jumping up and down, recounting unforgettable plays of the night and smiling in satisfaction as our rivals exited the gym in one glum mass. Proud parents swept their daughters into their arms for a hug and a photo—Mom included.

"Girls, you were fantastic out there!" She embraced Leah and Taylor, ignoring their sweat brushing against her skin like she always did. The fatigue on their face from moments ago washed away with pride. "Allie," Mom said, putting a hand on my arm. "You'll be out there again soon enough." Her eyes suddenly roamed the gym with a frown. No doubt she was still peeved at the principal and athletics' director for enforcing tonight's game suspension. I could hear her grumbling disbelief again at their unfair and impulsive decision.

Mom might be hot tempered and unforgiving, but no one could fault her devotion to her daughters—especially when it came to watching our basketball games all these years with Dad so far away. Even as a working, single mom, she rarely missed a game. When I was benched, she intended to turn in Shane and Tara herself, but I begged her not to, explaining that she'd be subjecting me to the status of a social pariah. That was far worse than suspension from one game, even a rival game.

I rotated my gaze, watching the gym unravel… but for the first time, I wasn't a part of the buzz—the excitement. Tara's heated words from that night at the hot tub came back to me. *"Where's that fire and drive you used to have? Did that part of you drown with your cousin?"* Her words hit me hard. I swallowed.

"I think I'm done."

"Oh, don't be silly," Mom said to me. "The suspension was for *one* game, I assure you. If they try to push anything else—"

"No, Mom, I mean… I'm done with basketball."

My words caught Leah and Taylor's attention, and then Tara's. She stepped away from Austin. All three teammates zeroed in on me, a chorus of confusion and questioning.

"What are you talking about?"

"Oh, come on, Allie, you're just mad. You can't mean that!"

"*Don't* do this, Allie."

The last sentence came from Tara, her breathing picking up in pace as she anticipated what I was about to do. "I didn't mean what I said that night at the hot tub. You've still got game. We need you!"

"Allie, honey, what's the matter?" Mom asked, touching my cheek to draw my focus. She seemed to search my eyes for tears and my face for emotions… as if trying to read where all this was coming from.

This time, I knew she wouldn't find the tears *or* emotions. Basketball—what I once lived and breathed for—no longer carried weight in my eyes after what I had survived. The burden of grief and guilt over Maddie's death had slowly but surely eased its way into a dominate part of my heart, sitting heavy and immovable. Basketball seemed a trivial concern in comparison.

I'd felt it the day I tried to quit at the beginning of the season. I'd pretended otherwise, but I still felt it now. Without another word, I pushed my way past my jovial teammates, making my way to the man who hadn't listened to me before, but who would hear me now.

"Coach Robbins," I interrupted, cutting him off from debriefing with his assistant.

He paused with a look of slight annoyance, though he acknowledged me. "Collins, what do you need?"

"Nothing at all, Coach. I just wanted to return something." I stripped my jersey off, leaving my green tank top underneath. Folding it in half, I handed it to him. "I won't need this anymore."

His mouth opened, and then his expression altered from surprise to his usual grimace. "Oh, for crying out loud. I don't have time for this, Collins." Coach Robbins pointed to the exit. "I'll see you tomorrow. And your ankle better be fixed by next Friday's game." He returned his attention to Jenkins.

He was making this easier than I thought. Why had I put up with him for so long?

"You don't seem to be hearing me, so I'll say it one last time," I said, aware that a crowd of curious teammates were creating a semi-circle around us. "*I. Quit.*" My fingers released my jersey and it flopped onto the court, a crumpled pile with no shape or form—merely the shell of an athlete.

I heard an encore of gasps and protests from my teammates. I saw the silent glare from my coach—but, more than anything, I felt torrential disappointment from them all.

I could have stayed and presented my case, defending my resign. I could have tried to explain how there was no room in my broken heart for basketball, but as athletes, they wouldn't be able to understand how superficial and trivial a win or loss seemed to me now. Instead, I let the stunned whispers behind me grow as I walked across the court, one last time, letting the double doors swing shut behind me.

CHAPTER THIRTEEN

The rumors from last weekend's hot tub bust came to an end. Everyone finally stopped spreading the stories and lies. In its place, the truth spread like wildfire.

"Allie quit."

For the first time in my life, I gave up the title of being a winner. Instead, I was branded with the taboo label for any athlete—a *quitter.*

"I still don't understand why you did it," Taylor said a couple of days later, scraping butter onto her toast. Each irritated, harsh spread of her knife left a growing pile of crisp crumbs on her plate. Taylor, like most people, assumed I'd come to my senses by now and "un-quit."

"I'm not asking you to understand," I said, glancing at the clock. "But I *would* like your support." I grabbed the car keys. "Hurry, we're going to be late for school."

"My support? Allie, you're *killing* our dream! It's supposed to be Leah, you, and me out there on that court! It's everything we talked about all summer!" She paused, looking at her feet, and then mumbling, "At least before Maddie died."

My emotions reared. "How could you possibly

even care about basketball this much?" My voice faltered, but I pushed through. "You were at her funeral, too! How has your perspective not changed? How is basketball still so important to you?"

Taylor's voice elevated to match mine. "How can you just give it all up?" she countered. "Maddie admired you for your talent. She wanted to grow up and be just like you—a confident, star athlete. And you're just throwing it all away. You're not honoring her by acting like nothing else matters!"

Her words cut deep, making me question my decision for the first time. Was she right? Was it important that I keep playing, even if my heart wasn't in it? We stared at each other, the impasse growing between us.

"I found my book! We can go—" Leah stopped short, eying the two of us. Her intuitive nature seemed to sense the heat between Taylor and me the moment she turned the corner into the kitchen. "What's going on?" she asked, the smile dropping from her expression.

Nobody spoke for a few moments, the tension building between us—an invisible, impenetrable wall. Taylor's scowl deepened. Her voice lowered. "We miss Maddie, too, Allie. Just because we're still passionate about basketball, that doesn't mean we aren't hurting. That doesn't mean we don't care!"

"Taylor, back off—" Leah started.

"You weren't there!" My sharp voice sliced through the air. "You weren't at the river. You didn't see Maddie fall in—you didn't see her bobbing around like a helpless doll in the water." My voice turned raspy. "You weren't the one that couldn't… that didn't…" I shut my eyes, fighting the images flashing through my mind.

Someone touched my arm. My eyes flew open. Leah's fingers wrapped around my forearm, her firm, yet gentle grip bringing me back. Taylor's scowl softened, though her arms remained crossed against her chest. Finally, the sharp edge of the car keys digging into my palm made me break the silence.

"We're late. Let's just go."

My day progressed with a sense of awkwardness about it, but the everyday interactions with my teachers and friends had to go on. Some people, my ex-teammates in particular, avoided me when we saw each other across the hall. Either that, or phone conversations and rummaging through backpacks often became super important the moment our paths crossed. I recognized it since I'd used the same excuse often enough. At the other end of the spectrum, other students made such a blatant effort to talk to me about anything *but* basketball that I tried not to cringe during the forced conversation. Why did my decision have to be such a big deal? At times, it was like ignoring "the elephant in the room". Although, my personal life seemed to have become one fat, overgrown elephant since school began, so it wasn't all that new, really.

Fighting the hesitancy, I sat with my group at lunch. We all tried to talk about anything but sports, even though we'd normally be discussing next week's tournament. At the ring of the bell, Shane pulled me aside. We really hadn't spent a lot of time together lately.

"Hey, are you going to be ok?" he asked.

I shrugged. "Yeah, I guess so. It'd help if everyone else was ok with my decision, instead of treating me like the black sheep of the group."

"No one's doing that," he tried to say, though we both caught Tara's glare as she passed by. She was still not talking to me. At lunch, she made a point of boisterously talking to Austin, keeping her back turned to me the entire time. "Ok, maybe some are… I think—" He stopped short.

"What?"

"Nothing."

"Whatever it is, just say it. Please."

Shane licked his lips. "I think people are mad and confused about your decision because they don't know where you're coming from. If this has something to do with your cousin… maybe you could explain—"

"I don't have to explain anything," I said, my defenses rising. We were about to breach uncharted territory, and I wasn't about to have that part of my personal life roaming around school unsupervised. Talking to Taylor and Leah this morning was about as close as I'd come to broaching the subject. "I don't want to talk about Maddie. No one will understand."

"Have you even tried?" Shane's irritation flashed in his brown eyes, meeting the sharpness of my own. The sudden intensity behind his words made me think he'd been holding back this conversation for quite some time.

"It's no one's business!"

"Well, maybe that's why you're standing alone in your decisions, Allie. If you feel like you're not supported right now, it's because you haven't given anyone a chance." For the first time, Shane's conversation with me took on truth and meaning. The seriousness of his words took me by surprise. Still, I took a step back, my obstinate nature kicking in.

"What? You really think if I tried to tell you about Maddie's death and how I'm feeling, that you would be up for that? That you wouldn't just try and kiss me to make me forget about it?" I was trying to make him mad so that he would walk away, but he still stood there. He ran a hand through his hair while he looked away for a moment, releasing a sigh. He softened his voice as he took my hand.

"Allie, I'm sorry. Forget I said anything." Bringing his lips to my cheek, he added, "Just know that I'm here for you—and I love you."

My hand slipped from his. My feet stepped backwards once more, widening our gap. "Wait, what?" I couldn't help the incredulous laugh that escaped my mouth.

Shane put his hands up. "Ok, hold on. Don't freak

out on me... That was poor timing on my part."

You think?

I cocked my head in confusion, my words faltering. "Shane, we talked about this. You told me from the beginning that we were just having fun. I can handle fun. I don't want to deal with—"

"Allie," Shane cut in, "I said 'I love you.' It wasn't a marriage proposal. I just meant I care about you. Why does that scare you so much?" He was breaking the rules, getting too close. I had enough emotions to sort through without worrying about Shane taking our relationship up a notch. What was the point when we were both graduating and moving on anyway?

"Shane—" I looked to the floor, shaking my head. "How can you say you love me? We barely know each other."

"I didn't mean anything by it—"

"Then why'd you say it? That's my point, Shane. People toss it around like it's no big deal. And really, this whole thing has just been—" I let out a sigh, shaking my head. How could I explain to him that everything about this school year felt like one pressure after another, including our relationship? There were some perks to being with him, but it would be unfair to string him along when my heart wasn't into it. Besides, if he was already throwing 'I love you's' at me, what else was he going to expect? Was he just building a platform for his intentions on graduation night?

The second bell rang. We were standing alone in

the hall and late to class.

"Allie, you are reading way too much into this—"

"Whether I am or not," I continued, "I just need to simplify my life right now, ok?" I hoped he understood what my words implied.

Shane clenched his jaw, his eyebrows pulling together. "Are you serious? You're ending this because I said 'I love you?'"

"No, it's not just that. Shane, I'm sorry… there's just so much going on right now and I'm trying to figure everything out—and I can't do that if I'm worrying about you and everyone else." The words sounded so selfish! And yet, I knew this was what I needed to do.

"Ok, look… I get it if you need to take some time to think things through. Christmas break is about to start. Maybe we just need to take a couple weeks off and start fresh—" Shane stopped talking when I shook my head. I didn't know how else to explain myself without being mean.

His expression tightened, like he understood I wasn't backing down on my decision. He put up his hands. "Fine. Whatever, Allie." Watching him leave, I felt a jolt in my stomach, not entirely sure I was making the right decision. I still cared about him.

"Wait, Shane—can't we please still be friends?"

"You can't have it both ways, Allie. I don't want to just be your friend." He retreated down the hall, but paused to turn around and say, "I hope one day you'll give somebody a chance, and stop shutting people out of your life."

I watched him leave until he rounded the corner. Then I slumped against the wall, feeling mean and small.

It felt so strange hearing the bell ring at the end of the school day and know I had nowhere to be. Out of years of habit, my feet took me a few steps towards the gym before I stopped myself. I stood for a moment, watching the athletes gather up their gym bag, the artists juggle their oversized portraits and canvases, and the drama crew waltzing their way to the auditorium for play rehearsal. Countless others linked arms with one another, moving with purpose. Everyone had a place to be, it seemed. However, I felt directionless. No basketball, no boyfriend, and I wasn't even sure about my friends… How had I turned my life upside down so fast? I fumbled for the keys in my purse, stalling with indecision.

"Ms. Collins," a familiar voice spoke beside me. I turned my head, finding Mr. Nordell at my side. His gentle eyes seemed to understand my stationary position. He glanced in the direction of the gym and then at my keys. "I hear you have some extra time on your hands."

"You heard about that, huh?" With a weak smile, I said, "You know, for a biology teacher who seems to keep to himself, you always know what's happening around this school."

His quiet chuckle highlighted the crow's feet

around his eyes. "Well, staying out of the attention doesn't mean not being involved or caring."

His words reminded me of the yearbook Tara's dad had shown us. I hesitated while he watched me, as if he knew something else was on my mind. "Can—can I ask you something?"

"Of course."

"It's about your life before Cynthia passed away."

Mr. Nordell nodded, not saying a word for a few moments. "Ok, but how about I buy you a cup of hot chocolate? I wouldn't mind warming up before braving that chilly weather outside." Perhaps he could sense that my question would not be a simple "yes or no" answer.

"Sure, thanks." We walked to the student-run café, its location close to the gym.

Seated at a small table with warm Styrofoam cups in our hands, Mr. Nordell prompted our discussion. "So, what is it you'd like to ask me?"

"I've been thinking about our last conversation when we talked about Yosemite and allowing change to run its course." My decision to quit basketball and my argument with Taylor this morning still weighed on my mind. I was trying to let that natural change happen by letting go of things that didn't seem to fit in my life anymore—including Shane, as bad as I felt about that—but what if my choices were wrong?

"Go on…"

"Well, not all change is good, right? What if life experiences change us in a bad way?"

"Ah," Mr. Nordell said with a raise of his finger, as if I had said something wise and profound. (That was highly doubtful, but he seemed inspired to share his thoughts, at least). "Your question seems to suggest that you have no control over that change—that life will twist and turn you according to nature's will alone. As foolish as it would be to say life doesn't change us, it would be equally foolish to believe that we don't have at least some say in how that change happens."

I wondered if he would mind the personal question forming in my mind. I took a risk. "I came across a yearbook from twenty years ago—the year before your wife passed away."

Mr. Nordell's expression shifted slightly, but he waited for me to continue, prompting with a mild, "And?"

"And… you seemed different than you are now. Like you were more outgoing—like you laughed a lot more. The pictures made it seem like you were really social and involved in everything. You were all over the yearbook." I had looked away shyly when I was offering my description of him. It was just an assumption. Now I returned my gaze to his, waiting for his confirmation.

Mr. Nordell nodded thoughtfully. "Yes, that was a long time ago. You are right, of course. I was quite caught up with all the school events and loved knowing so many students." He paused, a small smile on his face as though reliving some of the memories. "Times have certainly changed. *I* changed," he emphasized. "But being less outgoing doesn't mean I've changed in a bad way. I made a choice."

"What choice was that?"

"I chose quality over quantity. I decided to focus on individuals rather than the large group as a whole. I used to be friends with all the students and teachers—yes, even with my bowties back then, too," he joked. I smiled, noting the blue-and-grey bowtie he sported today and thinking that at least this one wasn't as hideous as some of his others were. I was afraid to picture what they looked like twenty years ago.

Mr. Nordell continued after taking a sip of his drink. "It's very hard to get personal with a crowd. Looking back, I have to admit there was a lot of superficial popularity behind it. Even as an adult."

I nodded my head in thought, though I was content to listen.

"After my wife died, I knew my path had changed. I decided my limited energy was better spent connecting deeper with a *few* people, rather than trying to befriend the entire school. It's what still works for me, ever since my sweet Cynthia died. What's really on your mind, Allie?"

This man seemed to know me well. There was something about him that I respected and admired every time we spoke. Maybe I could trust him—soon. I didn't want to go into details today, but I settled for, "I don't feel confident in my decisions. Maybe quitting basketball is giving into my grief, rather than fighting it."

Mr. Nordell took my hand in both of his with a

tender squeeze. "My dear, grief isn't a battle you fight. You must embrace it! It is a part of you now—it's Yosemite forming inside you. Give it time. As for basketball, I can't tell you what's right or wrong. That is a personal decision. You'll feel it in your heart what you need to do. Perhaps you already did."

CHAPTER FOURTEEN

News spread quickly about my break up with Shane, even though school was not in session. I could only imagine the hopeful, young girls everywhere flocking to virtually comfort him through Facebook and texts. It was a pretty glum start to Christmas break, though I was relieved not to be trapped inside school walls.

Leah and Taylor approached me, their expressions distraught.

"Shane hooked up with Crystal Jennings Friday night!" Taylor threw her hands up in the air. "It's only been two days since Christmas break started. Can you believe it?"

I continued slicing my pear on the cutting board. "Do I know who that is?" I asked, trying to keep my expression indifferent.

"Oh, come on," Leah said, "You know exactly who she is. Jet-black hair… eye makeup like a raccoon? Hooks up with a new guy every other weekend?"

I offered my bowl of pears to my sisters and bit into a sliver. "Ok, yeah, I know who you're talking about," I said with fruit in my mouth.

"Why aren't you upset?" Taylor asked, her eyes wide. "What's it been—a few days since you broke up?"

I shrugged. "We broke up. It's his right to kiss whoever he wants." Truthfully, the thought of Shane kissing Crystal, of all people, did irritate me more than I thought it should. I wasn't looking forward to seeing the smug satisfaction on her face when school started up again.

Leah's disgust presented itself with a scowl. "And to think we liked him…"

"You had crushes on him," I corrected. "You didn't know anything about him. To be honest, I'm not surprised. It's the party boy in Shane. The guy runs on thrills and impulse. Anyway, I'm not angry about it."

Taylor tilted her head and eyed me with scrutiny. Leah put her hands on her hips.

"Ok, fine," I admitted, tossing the empty bowl into the sink. "It bothers me a little. I just didn't want to say anything because it's not like I was a good girlfriend to him anyway. I was sort of one foot in, one foot out the whole time." I knew it *shouldn't* bother me, but I couldn't help but feel a little bit jealous… and grossed out that his rebound was with Crystal.

"Well, you can do better, anyway," Leah said, and then she sighed. "He's just really, *really*, good looking!"

I laughed, while Taylor grumbled, "That's the problem with all the hot guys. They all know they're hot, so relationships are no big deal to them because they can get somebody else just like that!" She snapped her fingers for emphasis. "You'll meet someone better, Allie."

Despite the hurtful circumstances, it felt good to be standing there in the kitchen with my sisters griping beside me. We were united once again, even if it would no longer be on a high school basketball court. It would still take some time to adjust, but I knew siding with me against Shane was their way of trying to show support.

"I'm not that worried about it," I said. "Boys are more trouble than they're worth."

On the last weekend of Christmas break, Leah, Taylor, and I stepped off the airplane, each slinging a duffle bag over our shoulder.

Leah inhaled. "Ahh, I love the smell of California!"

Taylor scoffed. "Leah, we're in the airport, which smells just as musky as any other!"

Leah didn't bother looking at our sister and maintained the smile on her face. "It's all about your attitude, Tay."

I wished I could feel as carefree as Leah right now. We didn't visit Danville more than a handful of times during the year. Our longest visit to our childhood hometown usually occurred over the summer, and even then, we spent a good portion of that time in our family cabin.

The thought of Hidden Pines put a damper on my already apprehensive mood. I muffled a sigh as we stepped out of the airport and felt the cool Oakland breeze touch our face. With Danville a small town of about fifty thousand, Oakland was the closest big city with an airport.

"Yes, we're here!" Leah said into the phone. "Yep, we're about to cross the street, so we'll look for you."

The familiar suburban pulled up alongside the curb designated for passenger pick-ups. Dad stepped out of the car, opening his arms to Leah and Taylor, who dropped their bags to run to him. I shifted my stance, my duffle bag still slung over my shoulder. A wave of guilt accompanied my reluctance to race for a hug.

I wished I felt as natural around him as my sisters did. They held no grudges against his past mistakes, even though his actions had cost us our family. Maybe it was because I was the oldest (even though I wasn't yet thirteen at the time) that caused me to hold onto my resentment and the memories of my broken-hearted mother. My sisters didn't seem to recall those details, or chose to move past them. Why couldn't I? Perhaps my inability to forgive my father had something to do with my inability to forgive myself.

I faced Dad, one hand on the strap of my duffle bag. The smile he gave me didn't match the questions in his eyes.

"Allison," he said, stepping towards me.

"Hi, Dad." Since I was still carrying my bag, we opted for a cordial side-hug. I gave a small smile, my lips pressed together. I could see Dad wanted to ask his questions—the same ones he'd been asking my sisters when I often became unavailable for his phone calls throughout this school year. These inquiries had little to do with our relationship and more to do with what happened at Hidden Pines last summer, and how I was handling it.

"Thank you for coming," Dad said. I nodded, adding a few polite phrases in response, and then followed my sisters into the suburban.

Leah and Taylor dominated the conversation in the car, filling Dad in on the latest highlights. They didn't mention Shane, or how I quit basketball, and Dad didn't ask—so I knew he'd already heard about both.

We stepped into Dad's new house, and I tried to bury my disappointment. This was the first time we weren't visiting our old home—the one I'd spent thirteen years of my life living in. I hated the thought of renters taking over our Danville home, pushing out our memories and making their own. But I couldn't blame Clara, Dad's new wife, for not wanting to live there.

A slender, petite woman stood behind the kitchen counter with her natural blond hair pinned back from her face with a clip.

"Hi, girls!" she greeted, removing the frilly apron from her waist. She hurried over, draping it on the couch as she passed by. Before I could decide the best way to greet her, she wrapped her arms around me for a quick, but tight hug.

"Allie," she said, her smile adding to her soft

features. "It's good to see you again." Surprised at the confidence behind her gesture, I could only smile politely.

"As for you girls," she continued, directing her attention to Leah and Taylor. "Thank you for simplifying the guessing game by cutting your hair differently!" They both laughed, completely used to the attention they received as twins. "Leah," Clara said, "this bob is so cute on you. I can't believe how much length you chopped off since I last saw you." She hugged both of my sisters and then accepted a kiss on the cheek from Dad.

Happiness touched his eyes, making them brighter than I'd seen them in a few years. While I wasn't thrilled last summer about accepting the complications of a stepfamily, I couldn't begrudge his newfound joy in marrying Clara. Now, as far as I was concerned, I had no interest in developing a motherly relationship with her—I had my own mother for that and simply considered Clara my father's new wife, rather than my stepmom. But Clara was nice enough, so I would at least be polite.

"Now that you're here, I wanted to tell you about your surprise." Dad pulled out his wallet and removed what appeared to be a handful of tickets.

"Movie tickets?" Leah asked.

"Concert tickets," Dad corrected. He handed one to each of us.

At a glance, Leah and Taylor started jumping up and down. "*Forever Delinquent*? Are you kidding me?" Leah squealed and then did an interesting dance of excitement with Taylor.

"What do you think, kiddo?" Dad asked me.

While I didn't love being called kiddo at seventeen, and I wasn't a fangirl like Leah and Taylor, I had to admit that tickets to this alternative rock band were pretty cool. Maybe this trip wouldn't be so bad after all.

"Well, I'll give you time to get settled," Dad said. "Nick and Aaron should be here just after dinner."

"Who's Aaron?" Taylor asked.

I didn't care about some kid named Aaron. I was more concerned with seeing my stepbrother, Nick Cross, again.

"Oh, that's Nick's best friend. Nick agreed to take you to the concert if Aaron could come, so I bought him a ticket, as well."

"Nick's taking us?" I wasn't sure I liked the sound of that.

"Well, it was either Nick takes you or your old dad here was going to chaperone. Which do you prefer?"

"Nick can take us," Leah and Taylor said in unison.

Leah laughed. "No offense, Dad, but it's not really your scene anyway!"

Dad nodded. "That's what I thought. Besides, it'll be fun for all of you to go out together. They'll be here for dinner, so I'll let you rest before your big night." Despite my differences with Dad, I couldn't fault him for always trying to please each of us.

When the front door opened around early evening, a blond-headed older teen entered first. The tips of his hair were bleached and gelled together, sticking up with an air of confidence. I squinted at him, assuming this was the Aaron Dad had mentioned. Wearing trendy jeans and a long-sleeved red and navy athletic polo, he led the way with a boyish grin on his face. Nick followed close behind, his hands in the pockets of his jeans.

Catching sight of Leah, Taylor, and me, Aaron's smile brightened. "Hey, how's it goin'?" Sticking out his hand, he shook mine with a strong grip. He moved along with his greetings, shaking each of our hands in turn. As he moved down the line, I watched him curiously. There wasn't an ounce of shyness in his demeanor. Within moments of meeting my sisters, conversation flowed naturally, especially at the mention of basketball. Apparently, he could play or at least shared Leah and Taylor's enthusiasm. I shifted a few steps away, avoiding their discussion.

My observations moved to Nick who, in contrast, was slouching in his black T-shirt. After Aaron's bold, friendly entrance, Nick's presence seemed to blend into the background. His energy level seemed only half of Aaron's at best. Nick caught my eye and, after an awkward moment of silence, lifted his chin at me with a quick nod. "What's up?" he asked, leaning his back against the wall.

I forced a tight smile. We had only met Nick once, but he was not the friendliest kid I'd ever met… Still, given the timing of Dad and Clara's wedding (less than a month after Maddie's drowning), I hadn't been an enthusiastic new stepsister either. I decided to try better this time.

"Hey. Guess it's been a while…"

Nick broke eye contact with me, his vision roaming elsewhere. I stopped talking.

Maybe not long enough, I thought. He didn't seem mad or annoyed. Just indifferent. Maybe that was one way we were both alike—not eager for superficial chitchat. I could deal with that.

With a shrug, my attention diverted back to Aaron. He'd made his way to the kitchen by now and was giving a high five to Clara, making a big deal about smelling her roast in the oven. I glanced back and forth between Aaron and Nick, who had wandered over to the fridge.

Did Dad say they were best friends? I couldn't have matched a more opposite duo.

CHAPTER FIFTEEN

Against my will, Leah and Taylor dragged me closer to the stage. It took some effort, weaving and bumping into bodies during the process. That was how I found myself surrounded by the deep throb of the bass, masking my ignored cries of protest. I had no idea where Nick and Aaron had disappeared. During our forty-five minute drive back into Oakland, Nick made it clear he had little interest in "babysitting" us. I had frowned at the insult, but couldn't agree more. The concert, held inside a popular arena, had been in full swing for an hour. The lead singer hollered into the microphone as the band broke into a new song.

"How's everybody *doing*?"

The crowd roared and cheered, appearing as black-and-white photographic blurs with each burst of the strobe lights. The band kicked it up a notch, playing their number one hit and causing frenzy. All around me, an eager swarm of bodies knocked into each other, jumping up and down and dancing to the upbeat tempo. I threw my arms up to my face, shielding myself from elbows and sweaty bodies jostling into me. Strong arms grabbed me from behind, wrapping around my waist and pulling me close to the rhythm of his body.

"Get—off me!" I demanded in disgust, struggling to twist away. He held me tighter, his body meshed up against mine. I threw an elbow into his side. He grunted, but this only seemed to fuel him. He laughed in my ear, pulling my body tighter against him.

"You heard her. Move it!" Whoever was behind me was yanked away from my back. I stumbled forward. A hand gripped my arm, steadying me. I looked up to see Aaron standing at my side. His height hovered over the crowd.

"You ok?" he had to yell, still holding my arm.

I nodded. My eyes searched the crowd for my sisters, who seemed to have drifted with the current of bouncing fans. The concert became like an ocean, the waves of people moving up and down, blocking my view and threatening to pull me under. On my tiptoes, I found Leah pinned between two much older guys. She, too, struggled to free herself. We had evidently underestimated the vigor of this concert.

"Can you help her?" I had to yell to Aaron. He paved the way without hesitation. In less than a minute, he reached Leah's side. I couldn't hear their words, but the brief altercation escalated to one guy shoving Aaron. Aaron shoved him back, knocking the guy to the ground. The second guy with thick biceps swung at Aaron's head. Aaron ducked, landing an uppercut to the guy's jaw. His head snapped back as he grunted.

The crowd cheered and taunted, circling around

and making them the center of attention. Leah tugged at Aaron's arm, trying to pull him away from the fight. The first guy rose to his feet, fists raised. He stared hard at Aaron. The other guy who had taken the hit massaged his jaw. He stepped closer. Aaron shielded Leah with his body, pushing her back into the crowd with one arm, while he kept his eyes on his opponents.

Two burly men in black T-shirts intervened. One grabbed Aaron by the collar of his polo and shoved him forwards. The other security guard directed the two guys who started the trouble, herding them forcefully towards the exit.

I had made my way to Aaron by now and heard him grumble, "Oh, come on..." I cringed, instantly feeling bad that Aaron was being kicked out for defending us.

As the band's hit number came to an end, the lead singer signaled to his band before speaking into the microphone. "How about a little love for you romantics out there?" Some of the crowd booed as the strobe lights came to a halt and the band transitioned to one of their slow, less popular love songs. However, the boos quickly blended with squealing from enthused females. The lead's warm, low voice emerged from the speakers, singing a calm melody with the keyboard. In spite of the momentary distress, the crowd submitted to the change in mood. Couples found each other, swaying together to the music.

Leah and Taylor stood at my side. "What do we do?" Leah asked, both she and Taylor watching the last of Aaron's form before he was nudged out the door. They also glanced back with longing at the stage. I looked around for Nick but didn't see him.

"Just stay together," I told my sisters, "and enjoy the concert. You guys deserve it. I'll be back." I pressed through the gentler crowd, making my exit.

Stepping outside, I looked around the vast parking lot surrounding the arena, but I didn't see him. I held my cell phone uselessly in my hands, realizing I didn't have his number. Or Nick's, for that matter—and I didn't want to call Dad and alarm him. I thought maybe Aaron had walked to the car but then remembered Nick had the keys… but maybe Aaron knew we would look for him there. Starting my brisk walk, I passed the endless rows of cars. I rubbed my arms against the cold, wishing I hadn't left my jacket in the car. Despite Northern California's winter feeling significantly warmer than December in Portland, the jacket would have been nice. My pace quickened.

"I see how it is," Aaron's voice interrupted the quiet night.

I jumped, turning around and punching his arm instinctively. He had been walking behind me, and I hadn't even known it. "You scared me!" Aaron glanced down at his bicep, almost laughing at my attempt to hurt him. He folded his arms with his chest puffed out.

"First, I heroically save your life," he said, "and then you send me into a brawl. Now I catch you sneaking away from it all." His face reflected disapproval. "Are you trying to get back at me for something?"

I, too, crossed my arms, mimicking his stance. "*First* of all," I emphasized, "I wouldn't exactly classify your help as 'saving my life'. Calling it 'heroic' might even be a stretch. Secondly, that brawl was nothing short of a cat-fight."

Aaron threw up his hands in exasperation, shaking his head with a laugh. "You gotta be kidding me!"

I let out a laugh of my own, so he knew I was joking. "Sorry about that. I appreciate your help with both my sister and me. How's your hand?" I asked, catching sight of his red knuckles.

He flexed his fingers with a shrug. "It's fine. I didn't hit him that hard."

Catching a spark of excitement in his eyes, I accused, "You loved it." Aaron grinned, his face lighting up.

"Yeah, maybe I did. Harmless fun!"

Glancing back at the concert in the distance, I commented, "I'm not so sure the guy you hit found it so harmless, but yeah, it could have been worse." I shivered against the cold.

Aaron seemed to noticed. "Well, you have a choice to make. Option one: you can ditch me and go back into the concert—"

I made a face and shook my head. "I was getting tired of the crowd anyway."

Aaron nodded. "Which leads to option two: do you want to grab something to eat?" He pointed to the fast food chains down the street.

"Sure, I could eat—"

"Or," Aaron interrupted. "A third option: I could teach you self-defense."

I raised an eyebrow. "What?"

"Self-defense. Considering how long it took you to notice I was following you, you're going to need it when you inevitably get mugged."

I let out a sound of derision. "Oh, please."

Aaron shrugged. "I have four little sisters. I wouldn't want any of them walking alone at night without knowing how to protect themselves."

He waited, as if giving me time to consider his offer. I let out a humored sound. "How about we just start with food and see what happens."

Ten minutes later, we both had burgers in our hands. Taking a bite, I waited for Aaron to finish texting Nick. After reading a follow up from Nick, he made a face.

"What?" I asked, wiping my face with a napkin.

"Oh, Nick's just pissed because he's 'stuck at the concert babysitting'. He found your sisters, so I told him to stay close. He'll get over it."

"He gets to listen to *Forever Delinquent*. I'd hardly consider that babysitting."

Aaron lifted his shoulders in dismissal and took a huge bite of his burger. "So, not to get too personal, but what's the deal with your parents? Nick doesn't say much when I ask him about it."

I put my burger down as my mind flipped through fragmented, unpleasant memories. Getting personal was not usually on my agenda, but I guess I owed Aaron a decent conversation since it was kind of my fault he was kicked out. Still, I must have been scowling because Aaron offered to take back the question.

"It's ok," I said. "Long story short, Dad had an affair a few years ago with some woman from work."

"Oh, man. That had to suck."

I grimaced in agreement.

"Your dad's a writer or something… did I get that right?"

"He's an editor, but he's also a writer on the side."

Aaron remained quiet, like he was waiting for me to continue speaking. I picked at my burger, drawn into the memories. "Sometimes Dad would lock himself in his den for hours, even on the weekends, with the excuse that he had a writing epiphany. Mom would get so fed up, especially when she'd just cooked dinner and wanted all of us at the table. Then one summer—just before I turned thirteen—Dad started working later hours at his office with the excuse that he was slammed with deadlines." I paused, playing with the napkin that I'd ripped to pieces as I spoke. "Turns out, he was hooking up with a co-worker."

"Man, I can't even imagine," Aaron commented. "My parents hardly ever fight."

I raised an eyebrow. He had to be joking.

"No, I'm being honest," he said. "Or if they used to,

it wasn't in front of us."

"How lucky for you…"

"I'm not bragging about it—"

"Mmm… you're kind of rubbing it in."

"No, I'm not," he continued. "I just can't relate that's all."

That's nothing new, I thought. But like with Shane and everyone else, it wasn't his fault. Our experiences were just different. And he *was* lucky that he couldn't relate.

"Anyway," I continued, wanting to move past the pity-card, "Dad's conscience got the better of him, and he told Mom about the affair at the end of the summer. After their big blow-up, he chose to leave. He rented an apartment or something. Then a couple months later, Dad started hanging around again, like he was trying to make it work with Mom." I paused, still able to hear Mom screaming at him on far too many nights to number. "But it was too late. Mom wanted nothing to do with him—said it was the 'catalyst to the inevitable'. That next summer, just before my freshman year, we moved to Portland."

"Why all the way to Portland?" Aaron asked.

"Mom has some relatives who help out from time to time."

"You must have been furious with your dad," Aaron guessed.

"Yeah, you could say that." I glanced at my phone in thought. My sisters and I hardly saw him that first year after my parents separated. Due to joint custody, Dad was entitled to more visits but he didn't want to force us. He hoped we'd visit more than we did. Leah and Taylor made a couple weekend trips without me, but I couldn't get past the hurt of his decision to cheat on Mom and then leave us like that.

Aaron seemed about to speak, so I stood up and gathered our trash, putting a not-so-subtle end to the conversation. It was a topic I avoided thinking about, let alone talking about. Fortunately, I didn't have to worry about our discussion moving forward. By the time I turned around, two girls had stopped to chat with Aaron, one of them sticking her butt out as she leaned on the table. Aaron spoke to them with ease, his naturally outgoing personality carrying the conversation. I could almost hear the flirtatious conversation resonating from his white smile.

The scenario reminded me of Shane and I couldn't help feeling sad about it, even though I knew our break up was the right thing. I shrugged inside, relieved for the interruption. Returning to the table, I interrupted the girl's playful words.

"Hey, the concert's about over. I'm gonna head back and find my sisters. Why don't you text Nick and meet us back at the car."

Aaron stood up. "Nah, I'm coming with you. We never did get around to the self-defense part."

"And… we're not going to. It's ok, really," I said, stepping towards the door. "Relax, I'm not going to get mugged. The arena is right there." I jerked my thumb, pointing behind me. It really wasn't a long walk. Aaron looked like he was about to protest. "I could use the alone time," I clarified. It wasn't in my nature to speak so openly, and I needed a break. Besides, he had company.

Aaron furrowed his eyebrows but conceded. "Ok, I'll see you soon." I felt his eyes follow me out the door. I used the walk to breathe in the fresh air, allowing the cool winter to chase away any negative childhood feelings resurfacing from my conversation. I was almost an adult now. It shouldn't still bother me… I decided I *wouldn't* let it bother me.

CHAPTER SIXTEEN

I emerged from my bedroom in a comfortable, loose T-shirt and fleece pajama pants. With a yawn, I waved at Dad, seated at the table with his laptop. Clara said hello from the kitchen, scrambling eggs over the stove.

"What magic pill do you take every night that gets you up and moving so early in the morning?" I asked, dropping my body with a huff onto the sectional couch. *My* early morning appearance had nothing to do with being motivated as an early riser. My body simply performed its usual torture of pestering me with unsettled dreams. They weren't even about Maddie most of the time, and not as vivid as the ones where I awoke screaming. My mind simply felt restless, filtering anxiety-ridden scenarios into dreams that didn't make any sense. On top of our late return from the concert, I felt beat.

I glanced at Dad. "Are you working?" I didn't know why I asked.

Dad laughed and scratched his brown head of hair, which was sticking up in random places in the back. "Yeah, that's the goal. I rose early this morning with what I thought was an epiphany, but turns out, it was nothing more than ongoing writer's block." He sighed.

Some things never changed.

Leah and Taylor emerged from their room down the hall only thirty minutes before Nick and Aaron. Like *normal* teenagers, all of them slept in. From my sleep-deprived position on the couch, I watched Nick and Aaron guzzle the last of the juice, eggs, and cinnamon rolls. They were like garbage disposals, inhaling all the leftovers. Clara beamed, and I couldn't help but be impressed by her cooking. Personally, I had inherited Mom's lack of culinary talent.

Aaron plopped down beside me on the couch, his movement knocking the book from my hand. "You came all the way up here to read, huh?" he asked, picking up my book and flipping clumsily through it.

I snatched it back, smoothing the bent pages. "At least I don't snore through closed doors."

Aaron threw his arms around the back of the couch, releasing an exaggerated sigh of contentment. "Well, nothing I can do about that. Gotta catch up on sleep when I can. Not a whole lot of that happening at UC Davis, if you know what I mean." He offered a sly grin.

"Gross…" I mumbled. I thought about Shane again, knowing this would be his life next fall—the hotshot college kid who drank too much, slept too little, and filled his time with a slew of other misdeeds I didn't want to know about. Not that Aaron fit this bill, exactly. I didn't know him enough to know for sure. It just made me wonder where I would fit in when it was my turn for college, assuming I made it through these final months of high school. I edged away from where Aaron's long arms were almost behind my head. We were the only two on the couch, so it was a little ridiculous that he was sitting that close to me.

"Yo, Jackson!" Nick entered the living room, tossing a basketball to Aaron. "How 'bout some ball?" Aaron caught it, palming the basketball in his hand. He jumped to his feet.

"You know I never say no to a game." He bounced the ball once. "But are you sure you want to start your day off with a loss like that?"

"Whatever, man." Nick knocked the ball from Aaron's hand. "Get your shoes on."

Aaron held the ball towards me. "Wanna play?"

Before I could respond, Nick interrupted. "I was just thinking a quick game of one-on-one, actually." He looked over at me and shrugged. "Sorry." He bent down to re-tie his shoelace.

Aaron squeezed the ball between his hands. "Well, maybe another time then. Your dad said you and your sisters were pretty good."

"For *girls'* basketball," Nick added. He wasn't even man enough to look me in the eyes with his insult. Instead, he fiddled with the lid to his water bottle. He was lucky my brain was too tired to retaliate at a normal speed.

"Nick, that's enough," Clara said from behind the

island in the kitchen. She put down the plate of eggs with an abrupt clatter and folded her arms, giving him a look that only mothers can master. The look suggested they'd covered this topic before.

Flicking my eyes back to my book, I mumbled, "It's fine. Wouldn't have wanted to play anyway." It was the first time I'd heard Clara raise her voice. She usually seemed so even-tempered. I knew her disapproval wouldn't change Nick's behavior though. For some reason, his actions were starting to escalate beyond our mutual indifference and I didn't know why.

Only one weekend, I told myself. I could make it through one weekend with Nick.

I did, in fact, survive Nick's presence. When Sunday morning arrived, Nick and Aaron packed up to return to the dorms, so I didn't need to put up with him for long. He didn't even pretend to say goodbye. Instead, he slipped out the front door and made his way to the Infinity Dad bought him as a college gift. I couldn't help thinking what nice timing it was for Nick to marry into Dad's generosity.

"Maybe I'll see you around some time," Aaron said to me. He pulled a hat over his head as he stood inside the frame of the front door.

"Yeah, maybe," I said, though I highly doubted that would happen any time soon. The next time I visited

Danville, I would ensure Nick was in the middle of finals or something to prevent any overlap.

"Well, if you ever need a babysitter for future concerts, you know who to call..."

I shoved his shoulder, pushing him out the door. "And this is where we say goodbye. Wouldn't want to keep you from your sophisticated college life." I tried to close the door on Aaron, but he caught the edge with his hand.

"Oh, come on, I'm only joking!"

I gave half a smile. "And I'm sure your sense of humor is a real hit with your late-night girlfriends. Good luck with that, by the way."

Aaron lifted his chin with a wide grin. "Luck is for amateurs. I can handle the ladies just fine without it." He chuckled as he sauntered down the porch steps. I shook my head, both repulsed and amused at the same time. "Take it easy, Allie," he called over his shoulder.

I watched him chat with Dad and Clara at the end of the driveway before I shrugged my shoulders and shut the door.

The part of the weekend that did seem unbearable was the visit from Uncle Bill and Aunt Heidi around noon. I'd anticipated seeing them at some point. They only lived ten minutes away from Dad, and it would have been weird *not* to see them. But I'd secretly hoped that I'd take on food poisoning or develop a sudden illness that would prevent me from coming out of my room. No such luck.

From inside my bedroom, I heard the doorbell

ring. My stomach knotted. I closed my eyes, wondering if I could feign a deep sleep. From outside the door, I heard their lively conversation. Everyone sounded happy, and I knew I shouldn't worry about seeing my aunt and uncle. Until we moved from Danville, they were a constant presence in our lives.

So was Maddie.

I knew that was the real reason I hesitated to see them—*only* them. Knowing my little cousin wouldn't come bounding from behind her parents and beating them for a hug caused a heavy pressure in my chest. On top of that, I couldn't help but remember the only hurtful words ever uttered by my aunt at the hospital. I knew she'd said them in a moment of agony. She had apologized later. But I couldn't completely erase the cutting words from my mind—because I believed them. I would always believe them.

Breathing deeply, I stepped out of the bedroom. Conversations came to a quiet halt as I appeared at the end of the hallway. Having opted out of the fall break visit with my dad, this was my first time seeing Uncle Bill and Aunt Heidi again since last summer. All eyes fell on me, and I felt heat rising from my neck and spreading through my cheeks. I swallowed, wishing I could dowse myself in water or disappear into the floor—anything to escape being the center of attention.

Leah, always the most sensitive to my emotions, quickly returned to her story, pulling Dad back into her conversation. Taylor jumped in, too. Light chatter began again as I made my way towards the couches.

My aunt and uncle stood and hurried towards me. Aunt Heidi reached me first, pulling me tightly against her. "I'm so glad you came this time," she murmured in my ear. She kept her hands on my shoulders when she stepped back, matching my gaze. She spoke each word with emphasis. "It's good to see you, Allie." With those few words and the embrace between us, I could feel how much she wanted me to believe her—to know that she didn't blame me for Maddie's drowning, even now.

My lip trembled, threatening to spill over into an ugly bucket-lip cry, but I turned it into a tight smile. "It's good to see you, too." I knew she saw the tears in my eyes. I knew she sensed my fight for control. She squeezed my hands and then passed me into Uncle Bill's embrace.

"How you doing, kid?" He kissed the top of my head.

After that, the worst of the weekend was over. In some ways, dreading it had been worse than the experience itself. We talked and laughed over lunch, with ESPN droning in the background for Uncle Bill. My heart lightened, and I enjoyed the next couple of hours before returning to Portland.

CHAPTER SEVENTEEN

With the start of a new semester, I stopped hanging out with my previous group of friends to avoid the awkwardness—as well as to steer clear of Crystal Jennings, who seemed to be hanging on Shane all the time now, wrapping her limbs around his torso whenever I walked passed. Apparently, their one-night-stand had evolved beyond that over Christmas break. I tried my best to ignore her.

Shane was just as bad. He smirked at me every time I walked past, or simply didn't smile at all, his unwavering efforts to make eye contact unnerving. I wished we could have still been friends, but that didn't seem to be in the cards.

As for Tara, we remained cordial enough, but our interactions were almost too polite, too shallow. Our conversations never surpassed a few sentences, both of our body language suggesting we had other places we'd rather be. I hardly saw her anymore though, since she continued to spend most of her time with Austin and basketball. With too many uncomfortable exchanges to avoid, the library became a frequent sanctuary for me once again.

As January pressed onwards, my extended time in the spotlight began to dim. My peers' conversations moved on to more enticing "breaking news," until my life was all but forgotten headlines. My heart felt relieved and yet at the same time, wistfully left wanting. In my fight to maintain my old identity, I seemed to have lost it all in one swoop. However, there was a sense of freedom in the manner that I'd given up basketball, a boyfriend, and friends who no longer fit the same way in my life. The choices were *mine*.

I started training again—but not for basketball and not for my teammates or sisters. Every day when I ran along the trails, bundled against the cold, I trained for *me*. However, the efforts to strengthen myself were less about building my muscles and lung capacity, and more about fortifying my sense of self. Dead leaves crunched beneath my shoes, sweeping behind me while I pounded the dirt. Rhythmically, I breathed in and out, absorbing nature's goodness and exhaling my stress, my confusion. I wished I had more to give back but, for now, I worked on my emotional cleanse. *Out with the bad, in with the good...*

As I ran, I felt myself letting go of some of my hurt and pain—just a little at a time. I wasn't sure I could talk about Maddie to anyone yet, even Mr. Nordell. There was still a well of guilt that I had to draw out of the abyss inside me—guilt that I didn't want to toil with, for fear that I may never step out of its grasp. Perhaps with time, during one of my frequent visits to chat with Mr. Nordell, I'd tell him why Maddie's death loomed over me—and the role I'd played and could never undo.

My phone rang. I stared at the name on the screen in confusion before I put the phone to my ear.

"Allie, please come get me..." Tara moaned through her end of the phone.

"Tara? What's going on?" I couldn't remember the last time she'd called me, let alone at nine PM on a Friday ni—

Oh. All questions in my mind came to a halt as I remembered the exclusive party I'd heard rumors about. I didn't know the details, since I was no longer part of the crowd invited to such events... If Tara sounded this bad already, I didn't know if I should be mad at her bad drinking decisions or more worried about her.

"Tara, how much did you drink?" I placed my book on the nightstand and hopped off the bed.

She moaned again before answering. "I didn't... well, I'm not drunk."

I rolled my eyes, glancing out my window at the snow-frosted ground. "If I'm leaving my nice, warm bed to go pick you up, the least you can do is be honest with me." Putting the phone on speaker, I pulled on a pair of tennis shoes, not caring that I was wearing sweatpants and a fitted T-shirt to complete my lazy ensemble.

"No, seriously, I promise," Tara mumbled. "I was feeling sick all day, but I didn't want to miss the party.

Just the flu or something… Thought it'd go away…"

"Where's Austin?"

"He's downstairs." I heard Tara pause to take a couple of deep breaths. "Said he'd take me home but… I don't… want to bother hi—" The sound of the phone clattering resonated into the phone, followed by retching noises. My own gag reflex struggled not to react.

"Tara? You ok?" I waited thirty seconds. After the toilet flushed, I heard her weary voice again.

"I'm here. I'm in the bathroom upstairs. Ugh…."

I zipped on a hooded, fleece jacket. "I'll be there soon. Just… keep your phone nearby in case you need help."

"You're the best, Allie," Tara murmured. Flu aside, she must have been a little buzzed to be calling me. And I hardly expected those words to come out of her mouth anytime soon, considering the grudge she'd been holding against me. Still, we'd been friends since freshman orientation when she befriended me as a new kid. Our differences aside, I couldn't refuse to help her. I wouldn't do that.

An alumnus from our high school named Darren Hills was hosting the party. He was one of our Pelican baseball stars who was drafted to play with a local minor league here in Portland a couple years ago. One of Austin's older brothers, Conner, was his best friend, which was why Austin (and the rest of the group) was invited to the party tonight.

Through the front door, I heard music blaring

from inside the house. Not eager to face a rowdy crowd of college students, I hesitated just a moment longer. The front door swung open.

"Allie! See, I told you I give perfect directions," Shane said, his voice carrying over the music. Not wanting to keep Tara on the phone, I had called Shane, and his instructions were surprisingly clear given his current condition. Shane pulled me inside the house and proceeded to embrace me with a big bear hug before swinging me around in a circle. My legs almost hit the couple loitering near the entrance.

"Ok, ok…" I said, prying his arms off me. "Put me down… yeah, thanks." I raised my eyebrows, surprised and unsure about this interaction. It was the first time he'd been friendly to me since I'd ended our relationship. Shane grinned too big, his eyes glossy and his cheeks flushed.

Leave it to alcohol to finally smooth over our break up…

"Glad you made it!" he said, throwing an arm around my shoulder. He eyed my attire. "And you dressed up for the occasion. Nice… "

I couldn't help but laugh, slightly humored. "Shane, I'm not here for the party. I'm here to pick up Tara, remember?" I scanned the room, recognizing a couple of alumni from two or three years ago, but most were strangers in their early twenties. Based on the liquor line up on the table, I was surprised Shane was coherent at all. I knew he wouldn't be before the night was over.

Shane took me upstairs, where I found Tara huddled in a corner with a hand to her head. Austin sat beside her with his eyes closed and his own head resting against the wall. With a drink in his hand, Austin didn't look much better than Tara did. I frowned in disgust. He couldn't have taken her home even if he had the decency to do so.

Tara opened her eyes, the olive-green hue standing out against her pale skin. I touched her heated forehead.

"Thanks for coming," she said.

"No problem. Can you stand up?" I put out my arms and helped Tara to her feet.

"Wait. Hold on…" Tara bolted into the bathroom behind her and slammed the door shut with more energy than she appeared capable. I wiggled the handle.

"Tara, the door's locked. Want me to come in?"

"No. Can you just wait a few minutes? I just need to sit here…"

I listened against the door but didn't hear her throw up yet. "Ok, but just for a minute and then I'm going to get you out of here." I kicked Austin's shoe, and he rolled his eyes open at me. "Go get Tara a bottle of water… and one for you," I added, taking the plastic cup from his hand and placing it on the floor. Austin groaned.

"Fine, whatever." I was surprised he complied, but glad I didn't have to deal with him for long.

Shane slapped Austin on the back as he passed us by. "Austin makes me look like a saint at these parties," he joked once we were alone.

"Let's not get carried away," I said, looking down at the party from my position on the landing. As one of the few underage drinkers, Austin did seem worse off than most of the others in my view.

"He's too competitive," Shane said, catching me eying Austin. "His brother challenged him to some drinking games. You remember Conner, right?" I remembered. He was an even bigger hotshot than his younger brother was, though Austin seemingly tried his best to surpass Conner's reputation. Shane chuckled, watching Austin stumble onto the couch, abandoning his assignment to find bottled water. "You can see how well that went."

"Oh, yeah, like you didn't play and lose a little, too." I shook my head.

"And there it is." Shane's smile disappeared.

"What?"

"Your look of disapproval. No one else gives me those looks quite as well as you do."

I furrowed my eyebrows, my mouth dropping open to argue. Shane's index finger touched my lips and he stepped towards me, closing the gap between us.

"I'm kidding." The corners of his lips turned up slightly, but he kept his gaze steady. "You were right to break up with me. It never would have worked between us for long, would it?"

I swallowed, giving a small shake of my head. Butterflies danced inside my stomach against my will.

Shane's finger slid from the top of my nose down along my profile and landed on my chin.

"The thing is," he continued, his face inching towards mine. "I kinda miss your face." His hand cupped beneath my jaw and he brought his lips to mine—too quickly for me to resist. I closed my eyes, the familiarity of his mouth drawing me in. His kiss was like a drug, fueling me with adrenaline and desire, masking sadness and loneliness. Maybe I could enjoy this feeling for a little longer. Maybe it wasn't such a bad thing…

A whiff of alcohol sharpened my senses.

My hand grabbed Shane's wrist. "Shane…" I breathed, interrupting his lips against mine. He persisted, trying to quiet my words. "Shane," I tried again.

'Hmm…?"

I pulled his hand away from my face and stepped aside from his cornering stance. His body turned towards me, following my escape.

"You're drunk." Considering the wooziness in my head, I wondered if I had any right to criticize his state of mind when his kiss had thrown me off balance with such force.

"No, I'm not." He tried again, bringing his forehead to mine with one hand touching the back of my neck. His words were soft. "I just… love you."

"Shane, come on…" I pulled away for good this time, his words snapping me out of his attractive trance. I didn't know what love was yet, but I knew it wasn't this feeling of uncertainty. "You and I aren't good for each other. You want someone you can have fun with—someone like Crystal…"

Shane scoffed, mumbling her name with a roll of his eyes.

I gave him a pointed look. "Is she here?"

"Of course not." He looked away momentarily. "I just wanted to make you jealous. I didn't need her here." His eyes returned to mine, pausing on my lips. "Why? Did it work?" Confidence touched his expression again, and he took another step towards me.

Jealous. Of course I'd been jealous. I didn't want to admit it, least of all to him, that a part of me missed being with Shane. Aside from almost getting arrested a couple of times, we'd had fun together.

But he wasn't what I needed right now. We'd been through this before.

I breathed through the flush in my cheeks, deciding to ignore the question he already knew the answer to. "Like you said before, it's your senior year. I am not the girl you want by your side, Shane."

His hand took mine. "Why don't you let me worry about that?"

I searched inside myself, fighting those persistent butterflies and feeling the warmth of his touch heating my skin. Was it so bad to get wrapped up in Shane again? Had my decision been too hasty?

Shane took my moment of silence to retrieve Austin's cup from the floor. He drained it. Catching me watching him, he tilted his head in question, waiting for my response.

I sighed and shook my head. Our needs were not the same. In some ways, we were too different.

"What?" he asked.

I took the empty cup from his hands and placed it on the banister. "You're a distraction, Shane. You help me forget. But I'm starting to realize…" I looked down at my hands, pondering and questioning the words I was about to say. My eyes met his with understanding. "I need to remember."

Shane frowned. "Remember what?"

I nodded, digging a little deeper inside. "Maddie. I need to remember and think about what happened that day. *Really* think about it." I remembered Mr. Nordell's words, likening my grief to Yosemite—allowing my grief to grow, and swell and change… until something beautiful and unexpected arose from it. "I need to focus on me, Shane, and not because someone is telling me to. It has to happen because I want to. And I think I'm almost ready."

Mr. Nordell's face popped into my mind. Last week, he had challenged me to try something out of my comfort zone. Now, to fulfill that task, I envisioned having that conversation with him about Maddie. Soon.

Shane scratched his head, his expression confused and with a shade of sudden hesitancy. He glanced down from the landing at the party below. This was obviously too heavy a topic for his Friday night.

I smiled at him, his reaction backing up my

decision. I could tell a part of Shane wanted to be the guy I needed… but he wasn't quite there yet. The rest of his carefree senior year awaited him. I put a hand on his arm. "It's ok, Shane. I know you said we can't be friends… but I'll see you around school, all right?"

Shane blew out a breath of air from his nose, looking me up and down. He appeared both guilty and relieved at the same time. His gaze lingered on my lips before connecting with my eyes again. "You are too pretty to go through all of this." He leaned in and kissed my cheek. "Definitely too pretty."

I pressed my lips together. "Bye, Shane."

CHAPTER EIGHTEEN

My sisters continued thriving on the basketball court, even as I sat on the bleachers beside Mom. She didn't understand my reasons, but she didn't push me about it either. I think Mom was relieved I wasn't hiding out in my room like I did at the beginning of the school year, so although she'd rather see me on the court next to my sisters, she knew things could be worse. A few months ago, they *had* been worse. Regardless, I didn't regret my decision to permanently bench myself from the game.

When the Sectional Championship arrived, it was weird being so far from the court. Even still, I could sense my teammates' restless nerves, and feel the anticipation of what it would mean to be champions. Last year, winning had been at our fingertips, and this was a chance to redeem it. Excitement aside, I also felt pressure, knowing that if they lost, the blame would fall on me for abandoning them. A part of me needed them to win so I wouldn't have one more thing to feel guilty about. Fortunately, Maya Walsh, the Tiger's point guard, was still recovering from surgery on her broken ankle. Now, my team might have the upper hand.

As the Pelicans and Tigers faced off on the court, I often found myself holding my breath. I watched anxiously beside Mom, having confidence that my sisters would perform their best—but anything could happen in a matter of seconds, including untimely fouls or missing important free throws in the last second, like I did last year.

The score board climbed evenly back and forth, keeping fans on their toes throughout the whole game. Mom and I squeezed hands, often jumping to our feet with the swift baskets from Taylor and Leah. Watching them move so fluidly together, I couldn't be more proud. In the final minutes, Mom and I screamed until we were hoarse, begging those key free throws to circle the ring and fall through the net.

We were two points behind. Seconds left, Leah retrieved the ball and made a shot from well beyond the three-point line. It swooshed through the net as the buzzer sounded.

The Pelicans won the Championship.

The gym erupted, exploding onto the basketball court with Pelican pride.

"You did it!" I swept from one sister to the next, wrapping my arms around them.

Exhaustion trailed down the side of their faces in streaks, but they both grinned. "We missed you out there, Allie," Leah said, after chugging half a bottle of Gatorade. The blue liquid dripped down her chin.

I shook my head. "Yeah, but you didn't need

me. You guys earned this all on your own." I hugged my sisters once more, and then released them to celebrate with their team.

The win wasn't important to me in the way it had been in the past. Instead, it simply made me happy to see my sisters' confidence and happiness grow, even without me by their side. It was good practice for when I left for college.

With the close of basketball season, the school year moved swiftly into March, bringing with it a rainy spring. On a particularly grey afternoon, I left campus at lunch to run to the store. I'd seen Mr. Nordell in between classes, wiping sweat from his brow with a handkerchief—something I had teased him about in the past. Who wanted to carry around sweat and snot in a cloth hidden inside your pocket anyway? At the store, I grabbed a box of tissue and a packet of flu medicine, just in case the changing weather was about to bring him down. I always broke out with a sweat and chills before suffering from the flu. I would keep my distance, of course—no one wants the flu—but from the looks of him, Mr. Nordell could use something to help him get through the last half of the day.

I returned to school. As I neared his classroom, I had to maneuver my way through the crowd of students in the hall. I checked my watch, confused by the bustle of kids hanging around. I knew the bell hadn't rung yet. Nearing Mr. Nordell's classroom, I could no longer mistaken the panicked energy buzzing the hallway. I'd felt it before—at the hospital. I heard the crying before I saw their faces—heard the words before I saw them spoken.

Get a teacher!

Call 911!

I barreled through the crowd, shoving my way past anxious students, their eyes wide and their cell phones open—texting, calling, taking pictures—I could only hope someone had called an ambulance because I knew what I was about to find.

Mr. Nordell laid in a heap on his back, his head lolled to the side and his legs crumpled together.

Too still.

A kid named Peter was checking his pulse, though he seemed to be going through the motions in a haze, as if he weren't sure what to do. Too many students were standing around, gawking, crying, unsure…

Principal Hayden's voice boomed from the hallway. "Move, move! Everybody out of the way!"

I beat him to Mr. Nordell, falling to my knees beside his body. Peter stepped away, visibly shaking.

"He's not breathing, I—I can't find a pulse," he said.

"No! No, please, no…" My hands grabbed Mr. Nordell's in mine, squeezing tightly. While mild warmth lingered to his touch, I could almost feel it seeping away with every moment that passed.

"Allie, step aside. Let me see him! Please, Allie—call an ambulance." Principal Hayden threw his phone into my hand, almost knocking me over. He gave two breaths, and then swiftly transitioned to pumping Mr. Nordell's chest. I came to my feet, my trembling hands touching 911 on the phone.

My breaths quickened in my chest. Too fast—I was breathing too fast. I felt my mind falling into a stupor, my knees threatening to buckle.

"911, what's your emergency? … Hello?"

"It's my teacher…" My voice cracked, my eyes falling shut. "I think he's dead."

I don't know what happened to the box of tissue or the flu medicine that I'd held in my hands. They were lost amongst the chaos with the crowd of students and teachers seeping into Mr. Nordell's classroom, shocked and too concerned to follow protocol. When the paramedics arrived, they strapped him to a gurney and sped him to the hospital.

Classes eventually resumed once the ambulance left, though school seemed more like a holding place to maintain a sense of order. I, for one, didn't learn anything for the rest of the day. I tuned out my teachers, who also seemed to be going through the motions. My heart beat fast in my chest as I chewed my fingernails. I felt an immense pressure growing in my chest. I watched the clock, waiting and wondering if miracles still happened.

Just before school ended, Principal Hayden called

me to his office to tell me Mr. Nordell didn't recover. He'd suffered a heart attack and was unable to be revived.

"I wanted to tell you personally," Principal Hayden said, "because I know the two of you were close. And given the circumstances of your cousin's death last summer..."

I stood up from my rigid position in the chair. "Thank you for telling me." Slinging my backpack over my shoulder, I bolted from his office. I dodged teachers and ignored my name. Escaping the administrative doors, I took off down the hall.

My stomach lurched when I heard the final bell suddenly ring. Students poured out of their classrooms, obstructing my path. I fought my way past them, bumping into shoulders and ignoring protests of annoyance. I thought I heard my name again but I pressed forward, refusing to look back.

A hand gripped my forearm, whipping me around and pulling me into his chest. Shane's arms wrapped securely around me. My backpack slipped to the floor, and I cried hard and loud. His hands pressed my head against his torso, and my body shook with sobs. I felt his hands caressing my hair—heard him murmuring words in attempt to quiet my tears.

"I'm so sorry about Nordell..." Shane's voice sounded far away.

In our embrace, my well of grief deepened, darkening with my despair. The images of Maddie that I fought to contain now rose to the surface next to Mr.

Nordell's ashen face. I couldn't see his kind brown eyes that offered me solace and hope. Instead, my memories of Mr. Nordell were tainted with how I found him in the classroom—death staring back at me.

"Hey…" Shane said after a minute, pulling back so he could look at my face. I hung my head, not wanting Shane or anyone to see my swollen eyes. At the sight of me, Shane sighed and pulled me close once again for another moment. I took a deep breath to clear the weight inside my chest, but it didn't go away. He grabbed my backpack with one hand and put his arm around my shoulders. "Come on," he said, "I'll take you home."

The school administration formally announced Mr. Nordell's death during a scheduled assembly the next morning. I almost didn't hear it because Mom tried to keep me from school, fearing it would be too much for me. But I couldn't stay at home with nothing to do. I was too afraid for the all the quiet time to myself.

When the first bell rang, teachers ushered students into the assembly hall. The room resonated with whispers, sniffles, and the sound of noses blowing through tissues. I learned that when death strikes, suddenly the deceased has friends he didn't even know about. Maintaining composure today, I couldn't help but scowl inside when I saw students, who had only ever referred to him as "Nerd-dell," wiping away a tear or two in conversation. Tara was one of them.

"It's just so horrible," she said from beside me, dabbing at her damp cheeks. Ever since I had picked her up at the party two weeks ago, she'd been talking to me again. She also seemed to finally understand that the world was not, in fact, over just because I quit the basketball team. Mr. Nordell's death seemed to ease this transition. Our relationship was on the mend. Today, though, bitterness infiltrated my mood.

You didn't even know him, I wanted to interrupt. I knew it wasn't fair to judge her, or any of the students who seemed upset, despite their shallow relationship with "the boring, old science teacher." Mr. Nordell's heart attack, which seemed to come out of nowhere, was a reminder of the fragility of life, warning everyone that death could happen at any time and to anyone. There was a time when even I thought of Mr. Nordell as "typical". Yet he wasn't typical at all—he was extraordinary. And now he was gone.

In what surely must be part of the school's code of conduct, handouts on grief circulated the classrooms that week. School counselors wandered the halls, keeping a sharp eye for students breaking down or suffering any kind of unusual emotion that they might attribute to grief. It might have been in my head, but I was pretty sure extra sets of eyes were watching me again and waiting for another breakdown. I could almost hear the questions bouncing off the halls.

Is Allie going to totally lose it? What will she do now?

I refused to be a grief project.

"How are you doing?" Shane said to me a few days later, finding me as I exited my history class. Since my breakdown in the hallway, he had been making frequent appearances in my life again.

I stifled a sigh. His question was well intended, but one I had grown to hate since last summer. There was no simple way to answer such a loaded question. Sometimes it was hard to know whether the question was a simple greeting or a true desire to know about the weighted thoughts and feelings constantly stirring my soul. Even if it were the latter, I had no desire to discuss the answer in a school hallway. I opted for a returned greeting.

"Hi, Shane." I released a small smile. I was glad he had been keeping our interactions casual. He seemed to finally understand that kissing me could not solve my problems or take away the root of my pain. But I liked the company, even when he often seemed uncomfortable because he didn't know what to say. We walked together for a minute, heading towards the open quad.

Crystal stepped into our path, her arms crossed. She tossed her head to swing her angled bangs out of her eyes. "Nice to see you two back together again," she said. She directed her attention at Shane. "Your explanation for suddenly being too busy for me makes sense now."

"We're not together," I said. Even though I stood a good four inches taller than she did, the bitter confidence in her stance made me feel small. She glared at me with her maroon-painted lips jutting out.

"I don't know what he sees in such a *good girl* like you," she said, looking me up and down. "It must get pretty dull." Her eyes gleamed. "Why do you think he hurried over to me so fast?"

"Crystal," Shane said, taking a step forward. He put a hand on her narrow shoulder. Her lips smiled sweetly at him, though her eyes darkened. Shane's face tightened. "You're gonna want to keep moving."

She let out a sickened laugh and knocked away his hand. "Oh, listen to you…" Crystal's attention diverted to a couple of her friends hanging on the sidelines. She waved her fingers at them. "Well, when you get bored again, just let me know. I'll be around." She tossed her head and flounced towards her friends.

I didn't care about Crystal, but I couldn't help thinking about her words. In some ways, she was right. I was an emotional burden to those around me, and I didn't have much to give in return.

"Sorry about that," Shane said. "You ok?"

I started to walk again, and Shane followed close to my side. My voice soft, I said, "Please don't ask me that… I never know what to say." My shoulders slumped, and I averted my eyes.

Grabbing my hand, Shane led me to a bench. He put an arm around me and I laid my head on his shoulder, breathing in the familiarity and comfort of his cologne. We sat together in silence for a minute—no questions. No words.

He was the first to speak again. "I never know what to say either… And I know you don't want a boyfriend, but I want to be your friend, Allie…" He squeezed my hand. "I'll be your friend."

CHAPTER NINETEEN

I attended Mr. Nordell's funeral, doing my best to merely observe respectfully and keep my emotions at bay. I tried to find comfort in the belief that he must be with his beloved Cynthia now. But even though I believed that, a selfish part of me didn't care. I wanted him here. *I* needed him, too.

As the weeks passed, a protective casing slid over me, sealing Maddie's and Mr. Nordell's deaths inside—and keeping everyone else out. I took again to the outdoors, though my rhythm changed. I ran fast, and I ran hard—so that when my body would tremble inside and out, and my lungs and throat burned, I could chalk it up to physical exhaustion alone and nothing more. Even when I became aware of Maddie's death tapping incessantly from inside me, seeking a way out, I'd seal the cracks and keep moving.

The call that summoned me to the counselor's office didn't surprise me. The school had to follow protocol. With a calm expression, I seated myself in the cushioned chair in front of her desk. Composure—it was all about keeping composure, so that Ms. Carol, with her pleated, blue skirt and high-buttoned yellow blouse, would have no reason to take notes.

She did anyway.

Smiling pleasantly, she asked, "Allie, how are you doing?"

"I'm fine." I tried to slouch in my seat a little to appear less tense.

"And how are you doing with school these days?" she asked, choosing to sit in an identical cushioned chair beside me, rather than behind her desk.

What a clever, calculated choice in seating, I thought. *Like we're buddies, so I might confide in you.*

"I'm sure you've looked at my records," I said, eying the computer on her desk. She wouldn't have called me in without checking my academic status. "I'm maintaining decent grades."

"Oh, well, that's wonderful!" She clasped her hands together in her lap, one manicured hand on top of the other. "It probably helps that you've had extra time on your hands without basketball this semester, am I right?" Ms. Carol appeared innocent with her question—but I knew she was fishing for a discussion.

I offered a noncommittal shrug.

She waited… and when it appeared that I had nothing more to say, she excused me to return to class.

Every week, Ms. Carol pulled me into her office for a few minutes, probing for something, *anything*, emotionally significant from me. I wouldn't budge. It was comical to see her own smooth exterior begin to fray with what I imagined was frustration. Her questions became more direct, and her hints more blatant. Her smile began to crack, along with the high pitch of her voice. It became somewhat of a game to me, and I found spiteful satisfaction in not letting her win.

Mr. Nordell would not be proud of my behavior. Sometimes, I could hear his voice in my head, a mumble of advice trapped inside a box. "Don't bury your growth beside me," he would say. "Yosemite wasn't built on sunshine alone. Storms are nourishment in disguise, and I promise they will pass." He would want me to talk to Ms. Carol, or somebody else that I could trust.

But I couldn't do it.

It had taken me far too long to trust in Mr. Nordell, and life—with its cruel tricks—had stolen him away from me just as I was about to reach the summit. I felt like I was tumbling down a mountain, ready to land on my face in a pile of discouragement.

Finally, a few weeks into the subtle interrogation, Ms. Carol asked me flat out if Mr. Nordell's death re-triggered the trauma from Maddie's drowning.

Her unexpectedly straightforward question knocked me off guard, and she almost had me for a moment. I felt the smallest fracture from within, aware of the tapping from Maddie's death drumming harder, louder. Ms. Carol seemed pleased, as if she could sense the slight change in my demeanor.

"Allie," Ms. Carol said, her voice softening. "You don't have to fight me on this. I'm just trying to help." When I said nothing, she continued. "You are about to graduate high school and enter the adult world on your own. You appear to be faring well enough—on the outside." She paused with her scrutinizing gaze. "But you will be by yourself, with no support. No one will know about Maddie, or Mr. Nordell, or your near drowning. You have a support system *now*. Please, won't you talk to me about what you're feeling?"

After a few moments, I interrupted the usual quiet that took place in between Ms. Carol's efforts to break me. "That's what I want."

Ms. Carol appeared hopeful. "What do you want? To talk about it?"

"For no one to know about Maddie, or any of it." At my contradictory words, Ms. Carol's expression dropped. I lowered my gaze. "I just—I don't want to be assessed anymore. I don't *want* to talk about what happened!" For the first time with Ms. Carol, my voice raised.

I was done. I wanted to be done.

Ms. Carol's hands returned to her lap as she quieted a sigh of defeat. "All right, Allie. If that's what you want, you can be done. I will trouble you no more." She stood up and rifled through a drawer in her desk. She pulled out a cheap, spiral-bound notebook that would surely unravel itself with time. "Just one last request," she said as I accepted the notebook. "You don't have to talk about it today, or tomorrow, or maybe ever. But all I ask is that you *write* about it. I'm not going to read it," she hurriedly added, waving her hand at me. "This notebook is for you. Just take some time this week to write down what happened last summer—every detail."

"What's the point?" I asked, flipping through the blank pages grudgingly.

"The point, Allie, is to get it out of your head." Ms. Carol opened the door, releasing me from her office one last time. "You are free to go."

"Allie, you've barely touched your food." Mom eyed me from her end of the dinner table that night. "How are you feeling?"

Scowling at the plate of frozen lasagna sitting in a mess of layers on my plate, I threw down my fork. It clanged against my dish. I let out a sound of frustration. "Why does everyone keep asking me that?"

I knew I was in trouble. I rested my forehead in one hand, clenching my teeth to control the rage of emotions bubbling up my throat.

It's not Mom's fault. It's not Mom's fault… I knew I shouldn't have been rude, and I was glad she wouldn't let me get away with it.

"Excuse me, young lady." Mom's tone silenced my sisters' conversation. I felt their gaze fall on me. "I'm sure your day has been a tough one, like the rest of them lately. Not that any of us would know since you won't talk to us…" The pause in her words accentuated the same disappointment that resonated with Ms. Carol's words. "But you will *not* take it out on your family."

I forced myself to look at Mom. Her fists held her silverware tightly in both hands. Behind the anger in her eyes, I caught a twinge of despair, exhibited near her tired crow's feet.

She was right. I wasn't being fair to my family. I needed to figure this out, for their sake and mine.

"I'm sorry," I said. "I'm really sorry, Mom."

She sighed, dropping her head. "Allie, what are we going to do with you?" She had spoken to her plate in a quiet voice, so I didn't respond to her question. She seemed to ask it enough that I knew there was no solution.

After a few moments, I said, "May I be excused? I need to work on something. It's… important."

Another sigh. And then she gestured with her weary hand. "Go on…"

Leah and Taylor raised their eyebrows in question. I shook my head in apology, not willing to disclose my assignment.

"I'll just be in my room."

I shut my bedroom door and locked it. Ms. Carol's words repeated in my mind, her instructions clear and terrifying. Unzipping my backpack, I pulled out the notebook she had given me. I ran my thumb along the plastic, spiral binding, grazing my fingernail along the edging with indecision. I stood up and sat down too many times to count, biting the end of my pen until the cap became irrevocably dented.

Finally, seated at my desk, I removed my head from my hands; I flipped the yellow cover open. I brought my damaged pen to the empty, white page—took a breath—and began to write…

Last Summer

CHAPTER TWENTY

"Can we rent a boat tomorrow?" Leah asked. She sat in the front seat next to Dad, her smile big and hopeful. After basketball, wakeboarding was the next best thing, and we were all eager to get back in the lake.

Dad nodded. "Absolutely! I can't wait to see the three of you out there again." The drive up the canyon—with evergreen trees stretching towards the clouds like skyscrapers—seemed particularly long that day, though it was only two hours from Dad's home in Danville. Every other year, Dad's side of the family met up at our cabin in Hidden Pines, located in the heart of the Sierra Nevadas in California. Dad's sister and her small family were already up there.

I jumped out of our suburban, arms open wide to receive the bullet of blond hair careening into my arms.

"Allie!" my nine-year-old cousin squealed, matching the eager grin on my face. She hurried to spread her hugs to Dad, Leah, and Taylor, but like a loyal pup, she returned to my side. "What took you guys so long? Come on, come on!" She tugged me along, barely pausing for me to sling the duffel bag over my shoulder.

Maddie announced our arrival to the open living room. I waved at Uncle Bill, who was reclined in the large, brown sectional watching sports on the flat screen. He hollered a friendly "Hello," accompanied with the wide smile that pushed out his double chin. Maddie plopped down beside him, leaning in and jabbering away. I was pretty sure by the look on Uncle Bill's face that her topic of conversation had nothing to do with sports—but he smiled and knuckled Maddie's head affectionately.

"Allie! Hi, dear!" Aunt Heidi peeked from around the corner of the kitchen. She wrapped her arms around me with a tight squeeze.

"Smells delicious, Aunt Heidi," I said, eying whatever was baking in the oven.

"You always have the best food!" Leah agreed, practically jumping up and down. One of the downsides of my parent's divorce was not living close to Aunt Heidi anymore. She often stopped by to drop off meals and treats that she'd been experimenting with. Mom could have used a lesson or two… or twenty. But we weren't about to say anything to her face about that. Taylor grabbed a homemade roll and sighed in satisfaction.

We spent most of Saturday on the lake, either wakeboarding or tubing. Maddie, who wasn't quite ready for wakeboarding, joined me on the tube.

"Ok, Uncle James," she said seriously to Dad, "I don't want you to take it easy on me. I can handle it." She flexed her fingers and readied her grip on the tube handles with resolution.

Dad hid a smile behind one hand, exchanging a humored glance with Uncle Bill. "Oh, I know you can handle it, Miss Maddie," Dad said. He exaggerated a whisper, pretending like I couldn't hear him. "It's *Allie* I'm worried about. I'm not sure she can hold on as long as you can."

I laughed with a shrug, playing along. "I'll do what I can."

"Allie can do *anything*," Maddie defended. "Come on, we're ready." She gave a nod, slightly shifting her position on her stomach. The tube swayed calmly in the water. I tightened my grip.

"Let's do it!" I exchanged a readied grin with Maddie, her eyes lighting up with anticipation. She loved a challenge, and Dad respected her zealous nature enough to give it to her. He jumped behind the wheel and the boat gradually pulled away, tightening the slack in the rope. As the boat gathered speed, we bumped along playfully. Maddie laughed into the wind, letting her hair fly crazily behind her. After a few minutes cruising easily on the water, Dad maneuvered the boat so that the tube slid across the wake, jolting our smooth ride.

I gritted my teeth to prevent biting my tongue. The boat picked up speed. Hitting turbulent water, we skidded across the water like skipping stones. My body swayed along the edge of the tube, threatening to knock me off. "You ok?" I yelled to Maddie, eventually noticing her playfulness replaced with intense concentration. Her arms trembled beneath her life vest, but she didn't answer.

I knew she would never want to admit defeat by signaling for Dad to stop.

I grunted as we hit the wake again. Dad was holding true to his promise of a challenge. I could see her strength wavering. In an effort to save Maddie's pride, I released my grip. The tube whipped out from under me, and I plummeted into the water with a painful smack. I popped back up, shaking water from my face, and watched the boat turn around to pick me up. When Dad slowed to a stop, he made a few playful jabs at my tubing skills, though his expression suggested he understood the intention behind my fall. He gave an approving nod.

My relationship with Dad always seemed easier when water was involved. I felt more natural around him at the lake than during our limited visits to Danville. Visiting him in our hometown only reminded me that we'd had to leave it behind because of his mistakes. That was another reason I loved Hidden Pines. The lodge was something of a safe haven—a collection of our best family vacations.

I clambered back onto the tube, rather ungracefully, in my waterlogged life jacket. "Not bad, sista!" Maddie accepted my high five, her blue eyes sparkling in the sunlight.

"Thanks, Allie," she whispered. I nudged her shoulder with mine.

"Anytime, Maddie. You know I got your back."

CHAPTER TWENTY-ONE

"Higher!" Maddie yelled down to me, pulling herself through the tree branches like a pro. Only a branch or two below her, I continued my ascent. Pinecones tugged on my hair and dry bark scraped against my skin. When Maddie finally halted her climb, I joined her on the sturdy branch. It was just far enough outside the pine tree that we could clearly see the lake before us, despite the dimming natural light. I eyed the grey clouds hovering in the distance and felt the chilly breeze shepherding them towards us.

Still, Maddie's face radiated bliss. We observed the quiet shore that had quickly been abandoned as the weather darkened. "I'm going to miss this tree," she said, inhaling the potent fragrance from the branches. I nodded my head, knowing exactly what she meant. It wasn't that this particular tree smelled any different than the other evergreens surrounding us, but this tree had history.

My sisters and I found this tree a few years ago. I was ten at the time. We liked it because it was part of a small cluster that grew close to the shoreline and was located half a mile from the cabins—not super far, but enough to get out of sight. If we ever wanted to escape our boring parents for a while, we'd take off running and play on our own. Of course, we did get in trouble sometimes—like the time Maddie was only five and was scrambling after us, trying to keep up with my sisters and me. She didn't climb very far, but she fell and fractured her wrist. It was after that summer that we promised to play together and not ditch Maddie just because she was seven years younger. This tree became a sort of clubhouse—without the actual "house" part, of course.

So it was no wonder that on our last day at Hidden Pines, Maddie and I found ourselves climbing one more time to take in the beautiful view and capture the fresh scent of nature drifting through the air. It was our tradition to say goodbye. I propped my back against the tree trunk, straddling the branch, and letting my right leg swing casually back and forth. Maddie faced me, balancing her position by holding onto the branches around her.

"What are you looking forward to this year?" I asked her.

"Gymnastics." Her smile broadened. "The beginning class is too easy now, so Mom said I can move up to the next level and go three times a week. By next summer, I will be almost as fast and strong as you!"

I laughed with a nod. "I'm sure you will." A few drops of rain hit me in the eye, and I wiped them away with my hand. "We need to get back soon." Maddie didn't even seem to notice the cooling breeze and the droplets dampening her shirt.

"What are *you* looking forward to?" she asked, returning the question. "All those boys that like you?" She puckered up her lips in a pretend smooch.

I kicked playfully at her leg, making a face. "Nah, not the boys. They're more trouble than they're worth." I wouldn't get into the details with my young cousin, but I had little intention of getting serious with anyone for a while. "Our basketball team is going to rock it this year, though. That's what I'm excited about." Running suicides to Coach's whistle, with my sneakers squeaking and sweat dripping onto the court, were not my favorite drills, but it was all worth it for the adrenaline of game day.

"You gonna be captain?" Maddie asked. "You should be, with your whole family on the court this year!"

"Maybe. I think so." After the thrill of Sectionals, I couldn't wait to play ball with my sisters again. It would definitely be a memorable tribute to my senior year. No other year would be able to compare.

Our conversation came to a halt when a sheet of rain showered us. The storm had moved fast. "Time to go!" I called to Maddie, making the first move down the tree. With a frown, she followed suit. Just as I reached the bottom, Maddie hopped down from her branch with a quick thud and took off running.

"Wait, where are you going?" I shouted, watching her movements take her away from the cabins.

"The river! Just one more time!" Maddie didn't even glance back to see if I followed. "Come on, Allie!

Hurry up!"

"Madison, don't run off." My words were more to myself than Maddie, who was far ahead of me. With only her giggle for a response, I picked up my pace, weaving in and out of trees and following the dancing head of blond hair. My shoes imprinted in the ground, the dirt already softening and giving way to the rain.

Our run lasted a couple minutes before I caught up with Maddie—or her shoes, rather. Having removed her sneakers, she was already stepping across the boulders, the uneven line creating a path from one side of the river to the other. It was a game we played every time we visited the river, racing to see who could cross first, but it didn't feel like a good idea right now.

"Hey, get back here! Didn't you notice it's raining? We can't play here today. It's not safe!"

I lunged to the embankment, swiping at her arm, but failing to catch her. Maddie only laughed, edging further along.

"You're going to get us both in trouble!" I had to yell over the loud drumming of the rain mingling with the roar of the river. I knew our parents wouldn't be happy, and as the older cousin, I would be blamed. Still, I couldn't help but smile at Maddie's determined energy.

I removed my shoes, setting them next to Maddie's, though it was pointless with how soaked I already was from head to toe—but that was part of our game to cross barefoot. I pulled my toe back from the chill of the water. "It's freezing!" My body shivered in objection, but I planted both feet in the icy river anyway.

Two arm's lengths away, Maddie laughed and said, "How much do you want to bet that I can make it all the way across to the other side and back?" Her hands rubbed at the water cascading down her face, her eyes blinking rapidly.

If she was going to cross, I intended to go with her. We'd both crossed the river a hundred times before, but today felt different—an air of warning lingering around us. As if to emphasize the worry in my stomach, my balance teetered and I almost slipped. Maddie, too, hesitated as the river forced her to regain footing. The confidence in her eyes dimmed.

"Madison, get back here! The current is too strong."

At last, Maddie seemed to agree with my assessment, eying the current rushing faster than we'd ever witnessed it before. Her lips pouted and she let out a huff of air, but at least she seemed to be listening now.

Wrapping my arms around myself to shelter my saturated body from the forceful wind, I watched Maddie pivot towards me. I glared against the bullets of rain targeting my skin. The game had lost its appeal. All I wanted was for Maddie and me to get out of the river, but I wasn't getting out without her.

My fingers reached for hers as I fought to withhold my stance against the river's pull. Her fingers close to grazing mine, I leaned forward, inches away from her.

Her foot slipped. I gasped as she disappeared

from my reach. She let out a fearful cry as the river fully submerged her little body.

"Maddie!" I screeched her name, propelling myself back onto the embankment. Barefoot, I chased after her, hurdling bushes and fallen branches—ignoring the sharp pain from debris puncturing my skin. I could still see her afloat, though at times the river briefly sucked her under before she popped back up to catch her breath.

She was young. She was strong. I had to believe she was going to make it—she just needed a little help. Losing sight of her again for a moment, panic tore at my stomach—but there she was, clinging to a boulder, eyes wide with fright.

Maddie was a fighter.

I uncurled my numbing fingers to grab hold of a branch, tugging it loose from where it had fallen into a bush. I bent over the river's edge, extending the branch like a lifeline.

"Allie! Allie, please help me!" Maddie's natural confidence disappeared with the river, and all that was left was a cold and terrified nine-year-old child. She threw out one arm in a desperate attempt to grab the branch. Her fingertips knocked the end of it before she returned her two-armed grasp around the boulder.

Kneeling on the embankment, I scooted my body forward, pushing the branch as far as I could reach. "Come on, Madison! You can do it! Just a little farther!" I hoped she couldn't hear the terror behind my instructions, my heart beating as loudly as the pounding rain.

With a leap of faith, Maddie thrust herself towards me, both hands grasping hold of the branch. A touch of terror left her eyes at the same time that I let out a breath of relief. Though the river still pulled, I held her securely, my grip on the branch steady and my determination strong. I had her. Everything would be ok.

As I attempted to pull Maddie towards me, my grip on the wet tree limb slipped. In my haste, I leaned forward to keep hold of the bough. With my body already at the very edge of the embankment, my impulsive movement flung me headfirst into the river.

Icy water swallowed me whole. The river stole my breath, numbing me with fear all over again. I shot my head out of the water, inhaling air and water. Flailing my arms, I fought to grab hold of something—anything—my body smashing into boulders in the process. I grunted, searching for Maddie.

Gasping, I spotted her bobbing a fair distance before me. She turned her head, blue eyes meeting mine for just a moment. Her cries were lost, whether because of my own gurgling shrieks or the sounds of the triumphant river whirling her around, I couldn't be sure. The river continued to dunk her up and down… until her little blond head failed to resurface.

My legs fought to find footing beneath me. My body twisted in vain. I inhaled as much water as I did oxygen, fatigue wrapping itself around my limbs, my mind. Thrown against the embankment, my arms tangled themselves in some brush. My fingers braided into the thick undergrowth, holding me in place while the river tugged on me, wrenching my body parallel.

Eyes barely open against the water rushing past my face, I caught glimpse of a figure above me. A murmured voice called out. I wanted to respond to the voice—wanted to see who it was… but I felt myself slipping, physically, mentally, giving in to the river's pull—until even the sound of the river's victorious roar was heard no more.

CHAPTER TWENTY-TWO

I lay curled on my side, my body half-inclined on the thin hospital mattress beneath me. My back faced the doorway, my position remaining immobile, as it had been for the past couple of hours. Casting my eyes downwards, I could still see the figure of a man hunched over in a chair near the foot of my bed, his head resting heavily in both of his hands—like he didn't have the strength to support it otherwise. Using the palms of his hands, he buried them into his eyes, rubbing away tears.

I shifted uncomfortably, just the tiniest bit of movement, but it alerted Dad's attention. "Allison," he spoke, his voice quiet as he attempted once again. "Please, honey—just talk to me."

My eyes closed as I swallowed the lump in my throat that refused to fully dissolve. I fought the tears, barely able to breathe. *Barely able to breathe…*

The river seemed to consume me all over again. Images of Maddie popped into my mind, her final look of terror staring back at me, punching me in the gut over and over.

I retched over the side of the bed, my empty stomach kicking my body into spasms. Dad jumped to his feet and hurried to my side, placing an uncertain hand on my back. He patted me awkwardly, probably grateful that I had nothing left in me since my previous hurling episode. He tried to hand me a cup of water, but I pushed his hand away, refusing his kindness.

I didn't deserve it.

Besides, the IV line stuck in my left arm should be doing its job. I ignored the irritating tug of the needle in my hand and remained on my side, curled up in the fetal position. The evening played out in my mind, accompanying the sick loss of control gnawing on my insides.

Maddie was gone.

They hadn't found her body yet but the search was still going on, combing the river, and searching the embankments for any signs of Maddie's survival—but she was presumed dead. It had been over four hours now since the "incident" occurred. My sense of time was a little skewed, though, since I awoke in the hospital bed with no memory of how I arrived there.

A nurse told me an anonymous person had brought me to the Emergency Room, leaving swiftly before anyone could ask him questions. All he had said as he handed me off was that I had almost drowned in the river. With the heavy rainstorm bringing in a surge of victims from other accidents, he had been able to slip away quickly in the chaos.

Lines of memory blurred together, leaving me unable to distinguish one from the other. I vaguely recalled being pulled from the river... and I had sensed that I was in a car, being taken to the hospital... but beyond that, I remembered nothing else of this anonymous rescuer, and had no idea why he chose to hide his identity.

What I did remember was the look on Aunt Heidi's face as she peered into my hospital room, her face swollen and red as though she'd been slapped repeatedly. What I will never forget, as I struggled with my words, is the wail that escaped her lips, her woeful eyes bearing down on me.

"*You were supposed to be watching her!*" The agonizing howl bent her in half as she gripped her stomach, ready to collapse. Uncle Bill rushed to her side, tugging her out the door. He glanced once in my direction, perhaps with a look of apology as our eyes met—but it was hard to tell with his face also puffy and stricken with grief.

It was then that I puked for the first time since I arrived at the hospital, wishing the agony and guilt sitting heavily in my gut would also be expelled. Dad had raced into my room, no doubt overhearing Aunt Heidi's words from the hallway. He had stepped out to call Mom, whose hysterical voice could be heard coming through the speaker on the cell phone.

That was about two hours before this latest episode of dry heaving.

"Is Aunt Heidi gone?" I managed to say, breaking through the dryness in my mouth. I didn't make eye contact with Dad, though I could see him from my peripheral, standing by the window.

"She's back at the cabin," he said, running a hand through his disheveled hair. He paused a moment. "You know she didn't mean what she said, right?"

I sighed, pulling my lips tightly together again. Whether Aunt Heidi meant to say it or not, she was right—I *was* supposed to be watching Maddie.

Dad shook his head, reading my thoughts through my expression. "She was just in shock," he excused, his voice pleading for me to believe him, like he understood the devastating weight of his sister's words. "She was still digesting the news. You know Heidi loves you, and it's not your fault, Allie."

What he didn't understand—what no one would know—is that it *was* my fault. I could have saved Maddie. She was within my grasp, holding tightly onto that branch—trusting that I would never let her go, but I did. I fell into the river, and I let her go.

My little cousin, my precious friend…

If Aunt Heidi hated me now, there was no way she'd ever even look at me again if she knew what I did. That would only make Maddie's death harder to accept if anyone knew that Maddie almost survived—that she *should* have survived if it weren't for my mistake.

It was then and there, in that confined hospital room, that I decided to withhold the details. It was better that no one knew. No one else needed to carry the burden of considering what might have been, or the burden of warding off my own personal guilt.

I would carry it alone.

CHAPTER TWENTY-THREE

They found her body the next morning—when first light and clear skies allowed for another thorough search. Even though we assumed yesterday that Maddie was gone, hearing the news that they had retrieved her body allowed another wave of heartbreaking reality to sweep through my family and me.

The way the TV reporters gobbled up and spread the news made me feel like a criminal, mentioning my near drowning while informing of Maddie's death. I'm sure every viewer wondered why I survived when she didn't—probably assuming I had only looked out for myself. It was just as well. I deserved the scrutiny.

In the cabin, I hid in my room, unable to face Aunt Heidi or Uncle Bill more than necessary. I was supposed to be packing up my belongings, preparing for our drive home that afternoon, but I couldn't do it. I sat on the edge of my bed, folding and unfolding one of Maddie's shirts that had found its way into my pile of laundry.

A tentative knock sounded at my door. Aunt Heidi met my gaze, the dark bags under her swollen eyes making me cringe. She had stayed up all night, waiting for the official news about her daughter.

"I want you to know," she started, faltering as her voice cracked, "that I don't blame you." She wiped her eyes, seating herself on the twin bed adjacent to mine—the same one Maddie often slept in for our "summer slumber parties."

I broke eye contact, still fumbling with the shirt between my fingers. I recalled her words at the hospital and the implication behind them. I didn't hold anything against her for pinning me as the source of her grief, even if she was trying to apologize for it now.

"You were like a sister to her," Aunt Heidi continued, her words low in her raspy throat. Her sniffling filled the room.

At the word "sister," my own eyes dampened again, and a physical pain compressed my heart.

What had I done?

"I'm sorry," I said, swallowing the burning lump in my throat. "I wish I had stopped her from crossing the river. I had no idea it was running that fast until I reached her."

"Come here, Allie." Aunt Heidi seated herself on my mattress, wrapping her arms around me and pulling my head onto her shoulder. We cried together for a minute more, the room suffocating us with the nonstop flow of heavy despair.

I needed to get out of there.

While the adults and my sisters continued to pack,

I slipped out my bedroom window, landing in the large parking lot. Despite our tragedy, Hidden Pines continued to move and fill the air with carefree laughter, oblivious to the screeching halt in my life—almost oblivious, that is. Stepping away from our cabin and heading towards a trail, I kept my eyes averted, sweeping the ground as I moved. Still, my peripheral caught the whispered voices, the pointed fingers... It was no secret that the Collins family would be the highlight of gossip this summer.

I walked for a couple of hours on a mostly secluded hike, distancing myself from my usual running trails, and in the complete opposite direction of the river. Never again did I want to see or hear the tormenting, mocking sounds from the river I once loved so much.

By the time I returned from my walk, my family was loading the last few bags into the trunk of our suburban. Aunt Heidi and Uncle Bill were already seated in their sedan. The motor was already running, as though they were anxious to escape Hidden Pines. I noticed my bag in Dad's hand. Someone had finished packing for me.

"We're just about to lock up," Dad said, gingerly touching my shoulder with his hand. "Go ahead and grab a seat." He opened the back door for me.

I looked back at forth between the two cars, eying the empty seat in Aunt Heidi and Uncle Bill's back row. A hit of reality stole my breath again. I shook my head slowly, back and forth.

Maddie should be here, like she always was—babbling away and insisting that I ride in her car. I marched towards the cabin, shoving the door open.

"Allie, where are you going?" Dad called after me, his footsteps following me into my bedroom. I looked around the empty room, less tidy than I normally left it. Candy wrappers lay crinkled on my nightstand, and the drawers remained half-opened, as though someone had rummaged through them.

"We can't go." My words were barely a whisper.

"What did you say?" Dad asked, leaning towards me. "Your sisters finished packing for you. I think they grabbed everything."

"No," I said, my eyes glazing over as I stared at Maddie's unkempt bed. "We can't leave without her." I sat down, gathering her pillow in my arms. Numbness crept up my body, from my toes to the top of my head, but not enough to deaden the pressure rising in my chest and crawling up my throat.

"Allison..." Dad held his hand up as though trying to keep whatever emotion was overcoming me at bay. "We need to go, honey." He put a hand on my arm, trying to pull me to my feet.

Something snapped inside of me—whatever was left of me to break.

"No!" I screamed. "We can't leave her!"

Dad tried to console me, wrapping his arms around me. I fought his restraint, screaming Maddie's name. I don't recall the details of the next few minutes, though I remember Dad scooping me up in his arms while I continued to sob and fight. Uncle Bill met Dad at the front door, his face alarmed.

"She's lost it," Dad tried to say under his breath, but I heard him perfectly clear.

Lost it. Lost her.

Lost Maddie—I let her die.

Dad and Uncle Bill continued to restrain me, all while forcefully buckling me into my seat.

"What should we do?"

"Is she going to be ok?" My sisters' teary voices echoed beside me from their seated positions in the suburban. Once strapped inside, my thrashing subsided, my face buried against the hard window. I exhaled shuddering breaths, embarrassed and exhausted.

As we drove through the twists and turns of the canyon and descended the mountain, I kept my eyes to the road, refusing to look back.

Present

CHAPTER TWENTY-FOUR

With trembling hands, I closed the notebook. The gnawed pen dropped from my grasp. Flexing my fingers, I rubbed the cramp in my right hand.

It was done. The lamp on my desk was probably the only light on in the house, since I had written well into the night. With a heavy yawn, I rubbed my eyes, feeling the burn of dried-up tears.

My counselor, Ms. Carol, didn't know what she was talking about. Maddie's story was written down, but it was very much still in my head, festering in a dark part of my soul. It would never be out of my head.

Not bothering to change into pajamas, I pulled back the covers and fell onto my bed. With a shuddering breath, I laid my aching head onto my pillow, but I was afraid to close my eyes—too afraid that what I had written would be relived in my nightmares.

I must have succumbed to sleep eventually because someone knocking on the door startled me awake. I trudged across the room and turned the lock. Mom stood there, cell phone in hand. I was glad she didn't still look mad from last night.

"Sorry, but your father called. He wants to talk to you about something." Her voice sounded terse, but I knew it wasn't directed at me.

Groggy, I accepted Mom's cell phone, taking a moment to flop back onto my bed. With my head against my pillow, I closed my eyes. "Hi, Dad. Why are you calling so early?"

Our conversation only lasted ten minutes but, by the end of it, I was on my feet, pacing the floor. My fingernails crept to my mouth, bringing back an old habit that I had kicked years ago.

Blackmail.

Dad's "proposal" was plain and simple blackmail. He had received word from the school about my unproductive counseling sessions (and by "received word," I knew that meant he'd been frequently inquiring, since I didn't talk to him that often). No doubt, he had also been talking to Mom and my sisters about my well-being, since he referenced how much I was running again. In his words, because I seemed "to be struggling with Maddie's death," he insisted that we spend the summer together—but not back in Danville. He wanted me to spend at least a month with him back at Hidden Pines. That wouldn't sound out of the ordinary, had last summer's event never occurred. But things had changed, and it was all recorded in that spiral notebook—a collection of pages that now seemed heavier than it looked.

"Are you insane?" I asked, anxiety building in my chest and creeping up my throat. "I'm never going back there."

"Your reaction is exactly why I want you to come with me," Dad said. "Before you go off to college, I need to know that you are taking care of yourself—that you're doing ok, despite what happened."

I don't know how many ways I said no, but he refused to budge. Finally, I said, "You can't make me go. What are you going to do, pull the 'money card'?"

There was silence on the other end for too long.

I gasped. "You are, aren't you? You're really going to withhold my college funding this year if I don't go?"

Dad tried to sugarcoat his response, like he was being a responsible father and blackmailing out of love. "I'm just trying to do what's best for you. I need to know that you can handle being on your own," he said again. "Besides, I'd like you, Leah, and Taylor to spend some more time with Clara and Nick anyway."

Nick would be there, too? Dad couldn't have planned a worse summer if he'd tried.

My conversation ended with me offering the silent treatment, knowing I had lost. I thought about rebelling and venturing to pay for college on my own—but I also knew that was a stupid move, long-term. A lot of kids would kill to have parents who could afford to send them through college. One month. Maybe I could handle one month. The thought sent me dry heaving over the trashcan beside my desk, thankful, (in between heaves), that last night's lasagna hadn't made its way down.

Rising to my feet, I stared at the full notebook. I opened the cover. Skimming the pages, I noticed how my writing transformed from legible to a frantic scrawl. A tear fell onto Maddie's name. I watched it leak across the letters. The ink smudged and then began to blur within the droplet of water.

Drowning them.

My chest heaved. I ripped out the first page. And then the second. In a frenzy, I tore the notebook apart, flinging paper across the room until the pieces of last summer lay in a jumbled mess.

It had been against my will when they tore me from the cabin, thrashing and screaming that we couldn't leave without Maddie—and now, it was against my will that they were bringing me back.

ACKNOWLEDGEMENTS

"Rumors" is the first story I've written with two very young kids at home, and it was more taxing than I anticipated. To my husband, Dan: Thank you for walking me through the entire storyline and letting me borrow your creative juices when mine were all dried up! The plot belongs to you, and I would still be staring at a blank screen without your advice and insight. Thanks for being my "Nordell!" Publishing would not be half as fun without you, including your self-proclaimed "shameless promoting" that is both embarrassing and tremendously endearing.

To my sister, Jen: Thank you for playing by my side during our years of sports together, and thus inspiring "The Collins Trio" relationship, and for nudging the conclusion to "Rumors" in the right direction.

I am grateful for my mother, my mother-in-law, Sandra, and my babysitter, Maicee, for giving me a break from diapers and tantrums, and allowing me time to write!

To my CTP team, Rebecca Gober, Marya Heiman, Courtney Nuckels, and Dyan Brown: Your ability to provide individual attention (with your distinct talents) to all of your authors impresses me to no end. Thank you for the challenge to write “Rumors”. We’ll see where we go from here.

Cynthia Shepp, I obviously haven’t learned from my previous grammar lessons from you! I’m appreciative for your knowledge and time—and whether I subconsciously meant to or not, thanks for letting me borrow your name for a character!

To my family, friends, and readers: Thanks for taking a chance on a new author! Your support and positive energy gives me confidence to continue writing.

ABOUT THE AUTHOR

Erica Kiefer was born on Christmas Eve in Southern California to an American father whose ancestors arrived from Europe during colonial times and a Thai mother who moved to the US during high school. Adding to her rich and varied heritage, Erica grew up living abroad in Asia, including Taiwan, Fiji, Thailand and Indonesia. She gained a great respect for the beautiful mosaic of cultures found in various parts of the world. After graduating from International School Bangkok, she attended Brigham Young University in Utah, where she earned a degree in Recreation Therapy. Her career as a Recreation Therapist has allowed her to work with at-risk youth since 2007.

Erica made the best decision of her life by marrying her husband in 2005 and is currently a mother of three, one of whom awaits her in heaven. Erica also loves singing, reading, writing, and satisfying her sweet tooth with chocolate-chip cookies.

CPSIA information can be obtained at www.ICGtesting.com
Printed in the USA
LVOW07s0716161114

413917LV00002BA/8/P

9 781940 534879